With It—For It—and Up Against It

Joel Cook

Copyright © 2006 by Joel Cook

With It—For It—and Up Against It
by Joel Cook

Printed in the United States of America

ISBN 1-60034-052-0

All rights reserved solely by the author. The author guarantees all contents are original and do not infringe upon the legal rights of any other person or work. No part of this book may be reproduced in any form without the permission of the author. The views expressed in this book are not necessarily those of the publisher.

Unless otherwise indicated, Bible quotations are taken from the King James Version. Copyright © 1972 by Thomas Nelson, Inc.

www.xulonpress.com

DEDICATION

This book is dedicated to my greatest source of encouragement, my beautiful sweet wife Deanna She never gave in, she never gave out and she never gave up on me.

ACKNOWLEDGMENTS

Special thanks to my very gracious and competent editor, Lu Ann Butler, and her meritorious mother, Jackie Hamilton. Without their dedicated labor and unfailing friendship this project would have been an object lesson in futility. I am equally grateful for the inspiration, guidance and support of our long time friends, Dr. James and Pam Burkett who kept me on track. Finally, I owe a huge debt of gratitude to Dr. David Remedios and Dr. William Noble, whose combined efforts got me over the hump.

Deanna and I are extremely grateful for the many years of generous financial support and faithful prayers of our friends and family, our splendid sons Kevin and Destin Cook and their families, John and Charlene Shepherd, Rev. Gary and Lora Mathews, Kenny and Bobby Nolan, Milton and Anice Fenley, Sheriff Tommy and Karen Denton, Rev. Phillip and Beth Strickland, Robert and Rachel Munoz, Gene and Donna White, Anna Wells, Esther Andrews,

With It—For It—and Up Against It

Dr. William and Dawn Noble, Dr. Stacy and Tami Cude, Rev. Dale and Jean Gentry, Luther and Jackie Hamilton, Jack and Delena Shelton, Jerry and Wanda Karr, Ed and Betty Wilson, Alan and Beverly Barrington, Janell Arndt, Greg and Gloria Kopycinski, Dr. Ray Lake, Ron and Jo Griffin, Al and Sue Laird, Bennie and Diane Reynolds, Ernest and Frankie Pate, Bo and Judy Johnson, Rev. Robert and Vicki Shipley, Dorthy Stanger, Honey Colburn, Keith and Sarah Hogden, Dora Jones, Steve and Kaye Neal, Rev. Gary and Diana Fletcher, Rev. Robert and Sharon Jones, Rev. Tommy and Mary Brown, Rev. Chris and Stephanie Welch, Rev. John and Linda Brewster, Rev. Bobby and Candy Hankins, Rev. Joe and Lynda Ragland, Rev. Mike and Kim Atherton, Rev. Jack and Dianne Smith, Rev. Tom and Mary Peters, Rev. Rick and Cindy Hester, Rev. Rusty and Anne Griffin, Rev. Charles and Faye Wigley, Rev. Kerry and Faith Wood, Rev. Harold and Marilyn Morton, Rev. Dan and Sarah Craig, Rev. Dan and Suzie Thompson, Rev. Paul and Perrianne Brownback, Rev. Bo and Cecilia Loftis, Rev. Mike and Brenda Amico.

A note of thanks to Rita Ardoin Debrow for her artistic efforts in this project.

With It—For It—and Up Against It

~~~

The morning air was alive with the lucrative sounds of the carnival midway. The fragrant aromas of popcorn, caramel apples and cotton candy wafted through the air as familiar as an old friend. Inside the popcorn trailer, Pete was stirring his secret caramel recipe in a huge copper kettle. Sweat rolled down his massive forearms as he stirred his guarded concoction with a large wooden paddle.

Agitatin' Bill was whistling in an off key way as he rolled the sidewall of the merry-go-round higher and higher, exposing the carefully refurbished carousel horses. It was opening day and it couldn't have come too quickly for him. The sounds of Glen Miller's band were struggling to be heard from a small radio he had plugged into an improvised light socket.

Winter Quarters was now a vague memory. The opening date on the spring schedule had finally arrived. Hope springs eternal, at least it's supposed to. One thing for sure, once you get sawdust in your veins, nothing can restrain the need to be 'with it'.

Johnny Palmer was hastily striding up the carnival midway. He had been with one carnival or another all of his life, or in the words of the old time carneys, "with it, for it and up against it", which meant he was with the carnival, for the carnival and up against anything that opposed the carnival. It was all he knew. It was all he ever wanted to know. It was a world that satisfied his need for cash, company and circumstance.

There were few rules governing the way of the carney. Thankfully, independence was the bedrock from which all actions are judged. You can do anything, within reason, you're big enough to do, if you exercise the outrageous ability to try. After all, this was the fifties, the war was over and America was palpitating with promise, passion and purpose. All you needed was the right route, the right gimmick, fair weather and a little bit of luck.

Life for the most part had been manageable. Now, in his early thirties, Johnny had known his moments. Women had always been around, along with the opportunity for hard living. For whatever reason, he seemed to be immune to the debilitating effects of life on the road.

As he headed toward the cookhouse, the movement of his six-foot frame seemed to be the conspired effort of a ballet dancer and top ranked boxer. His thick dark hair showed little sign of thinning. His brown eyes, when observed by others, were best described as compelling and captivating. The corners

With It—For It—and Up Against It

of his mouth were always poised to celebrate the challenges of life with sounds of merriment. Yet, there was about him an incendiary attitude. When provoked he could be quite calculating and dangerous.

He had been making it on his own for a long time now. Like all carneys, he knew the rhythm and roll of being shut down one day and running wide open the next. The lot (land or location where carneys work and most live) was no place for the lazy or the needy. There was no welfare plan or no community care. It was do or die; if you didn't work, you didn't eat. Oh, there was help for the helpless. The brotherhood of showman could be most benevolent when it was deserved. Taking care of their own was a necessary part of the business. However, they had no tolerance for abusers, bums or backstabbers. Justice, though rare, was sudden and sufficient.

The call (time listed to open midway) had been lettered on the office trailer blackboard. "We spring (we open at a certain hour) at 6 o' clock," commented a small sickly man, known only as Easy Money, as Johnny sat down at Bill Charity's cookhouse counter next to his best friend, Happy Parks. Happy's name best described his jovial personality —he was always happy. At first glance his appearance could be deceiving; he was tattooed from head to toe. In the circus sideshow he had been known as "The Illustrated Man." Now five years later, he was the successful owner and operator of a very profitable penny arcade.

A bachelor, like Johnny, he cheerfully claimed he wasn't married because no one would have him.

Johnny figured one excuse was as good as another. "Well, at least the lot's dry," Happy observed as he got up to leave. Johnny said goodbye to his friend and ordered a cup of black coffee.

Most spring dates attracted foul weather and small crowds. On occasion good money was to be made but for the most part previewing and preparing the rides and shows for the fair circuit was uppermost in the minds of the carnival staff.

Johnny nursed his coffee and thought about his own prospects for the season. He had acquired a 1949 Roadmaster Buick and a deceptively clean repossessed Spartan house trailer. The escalating costs of hotel rooms, cab fares and other expenditures had encouraged change. Living on the lot had its advantages, especially in times of high winds and hail. Bad storms had wiped out more than a few carnivals over the years. He could ill afford any kind of catastrophe at this point and time. Carneys always paid cash for any and all purchases, so spring had found him carrying a thin bankroll.

He had booked an array of joints. Always the optimist, he had setup and flashed (placing the prizes in the most enticing location) a cork gallery (air rifles fire corks at targets), a balloon joint (darts are thrown at balloons) and a six cat (baseballs are thrown at cat looking targets.) The privilege (amount of money paid the show owner for privilege of doing business) was reasonable enough but he knew it was real easy to wind up in a donniker (rest room or any kind of crappie place to do business) location because of past due accounts in the Mighty Wright office trailer.

With It—For It—and Up Against It

To his credit, he had control over most of his bad habits. Time and trouble had been his teacher. Wisdom never partners with the pampered. He had learned to manage his money, his mind and his manner.

Presently, his thoughts were interrupted by an incessant flow of filthy words that identified the ride superintendent (supervisor of all show owned rides) who always had a beef with somebody. The bearer of these observations of agitation was a thick chested, heavily muscled intimidator known as Pollock. His huge fists hammered the counter as he inquired, "Whatta ya gotta do to get a cup of coffee around here?"

With a slow easy motion, Johnny set his coffee cup on the counter and decided to direct his conversation toward someone who was using more than half of his brain. "Hey, Easy Money, are all the junction boxes hot?"

"As far as I know," he replied. "Willie, (the show electrician), was dragging the last of the cable toward the rock-o-plane a couple of hours ago."

Johnny purposely avoided any conversation with Pollock. He had more than a few reasons to dislike the loud-mouthed predator. Last summer, in the G top, (gambling tent behind midway for carneys only) one of Johnny's six-cat agents had been beaten unconscious during a knock rummy game. By all accounts the attack was unprovoked. The huge lumbering ride superintendent had little if any skill in card games. The only outlet for his frustration was the sadistic infliction of pain and misery imposed upon others.

One of the participants present that day had to be physically restrained or Pollock would have been the

With It—For It—and Up Against It

recipient of a full compliment of 38 slugs. After all, this wasn't a nursery class. There were more than a few practitioners of gambler etiquette. If money is important, don't play.

There was a general feeling up and down the midway that it wouldn't have been a great loss if those 38 slugs had been allowed to speak.

A newcomer might have wondered how he kept his job. It was common knowledge that Dixie Wright, the show owner's young wife, was engaged in an illicit affair that thrived on the brutality of the big Pollock. To his credit, the show moved with precise order and safety. He knew his job, and more and more, the benefits were measured in increments not limited to money alone.

A sarcastic tone cut through his thinking, as the big Pollock boomed out, "Palmer! You're gonna have to move your stock truck. It's blocking the fire lane behind the funhouse, so get it moved within the hour." Everyone knew there wasn't any backside fire lane, especially on a still date.

It wasn't the first time Johnny had faced the conspicuous belligerence of this tarnished tyrant. "I'll see what I can do," he replied coolly, as he stood and walked outside. Experience had taught him to hide any response that might disclose his inner thoughts. He had observed in others the futility of indulging in hatred and animosity. It could kill you quicker than a heart attack. It was a good idea to avoid exercises in futility.

Johnny was his own man. He had nothing to prove. Self assured and confident, he was not impressed or

With It—For It—and Up Against It

intimidated by anyone, including Pollock. Acts of aggression always find an opportune hour. He and Pollock were gonna dance. The time and the tune would be on his terms, and he was happy to wait for an advantage.

Moving the stock truck (storage for plush teddy bears etc. slum-cheap prizes, also food products) wasn't much of an inconvenience; the intentions behind the instructions were another matter. For now, he would comply. The expense of a "roughie" (sets up and tears down joints and does maintenance) was impractical at this time, so Johnny spent the afternoon tidying up around the front of his joints. The local dump trucks were spreading wood shaving down the center of the midway, activity increased up and down the lot as 6 o'clock drew near.

Johnny removed his shirt as beads of sweat gathered on his darkly tanned back. It is not uncommon for a 16-pound sledgehammer to generate moisture. The tent stakes were quickly driven in the ground as the sledgehammer fell in fluid powerful strokes. It was good to hear the sound of metal against metal.

The afternoon sun descended over the contours of his surprisingly symmetrical broad shoulders and tapering waist. His muscles were long and well formed. Somehow he had avoided the tattoo needles but there were other marks that were not considered works of art. Most prominent was a scar, long and thin, that had been inscribed on the left side of his back. There was a wild story that included a knife. It was a safe bet it had occurred somewhere other than

With It—For It—and Up Against It

a Sunday school class. For the most part though, his body was unscathed.

At precisely 6 o'clock the amplified sounds of organ music, generated from the antiquated German-built jenny, (merry-go-round) announced with melodic certainty the beginning of the new season. The Mighty Wright Shows was open!

Nancy Wright, sister to the show owner Malcolm Wright, was headed toward the merry-go-round ticket box, also known as Double Bottom's plantation. She had sat in the confines of that small cubicle for more years than anyone could imagine. Large quantities of junk food, a minimum amount of movement and gravity's tireless tug had produced a posterior of gigantic proportions.

She was a sad figure; lost love had been her undoing. The man of memory had been a poor choice. He had stolen more than just her love. A lifetime of savings had been taken along with another man's wife. To this day his whereabouts are unknown. Nancy placated her unrequited love with a daily drained fifth of cheap gin. Everyone knew it. They also knew Malcolm Wright didn't want to hear about it.

Through the front gate a few people begin to trickle down the midway. In every spot you always have a handful of folks who come early, stay late and spend little. In the language of the carney, they are known as lot lice. This is not a term of contempt but one way of identifying part of the crowd.

Night had fallen. The midway, in spectacular fashion, took on a new personality. The outbursting splendor of light and sound can mesmerize the sensibilities of the masses. The opening night crowd had arrived in large number, and even more surprising, they were spending money.

The rides were busy and the concessions were experiencing activity as well. The night was alive with the squeals of dread and delight as thrilled passengers echoed their apprehension and approval.

Johnny tied a nail apron, full of change, around his narrow waist, jumped over the counter of the balloon joint and called out, "How about you, Lucky? Three darts for a quarter. Step on in here and win a big one. Make the little lady happy." Before long he had a good tip going. Balloons were bursting, players were celebrating, money was flowing, life was good.

As quickly as the midway filled, just that quickly it emptied. These were working people with kids in school. It was bedtime. The long line of automobiles leaving the parking lot testified to this truth.

Surprised at the success of opening night, Johnny realized his need to hire some more help, especially agents. He had not been able to keep an eye on his other joints. His agent on the cork gallery had been with him a number of years. He knew Johnny could check the inventory and have an idea how much money had changed hands.

The six cat was a different matter. Of the four agents, three were new. In ideal conditions it was next to impossible to prevent the agents from having first count on the money. Little if any stock had been thrown. The wise concessionaire sought to keep the skimming (taking money that doesn't belong to you) to a minimum. Learning this lesson hadn't been

With It—For It—and Up Against It

cheap. Keeping everyone honest was impossible. He did the best he could.

The last of the awnings were being laced as Johnny gathered the night's take and headed toward the trailer. The midway was enveloped in a disenchanting silence. It was hard to explain the melancholy atmosphere that hovered in the heavy night air.

The night's exhilaration and merriment had subsided. You could still smell the sweet fragrance of cotton candy and other wonderful delights. It was all a part of the sawdust trail's seductive influence. It was magical! Few could resist its charm.

Down in the hot wagon, (semi-trailer that houses stationary engines that generate electricity) Willie was powering down the big caterpillar engines. There would be little need for large amounts of electricity at this late hour.

Discarded trash littered the ground. Tomorrow morning the midway would be cleaned and raked. Some of the old-timers would be out early scanning the ground, especially under the shake rides, (shakes money and other objects out of riders' pockets) looking for money, jewelry, billfolds and anything of value. The finds were often numerous.

In a practiced unsteady gait, Double Bottom headed toward the office trailer. Many of the ticket sellers were already lined up at the checkout window. The accounting consisted in subtracting the ending number from the starting ticket number, which determined the amount of money made. Most ticket sellers were seldom short. There would usually be extra cash, called walks. Walks occur when the purchaser,

With It—For It—and Up Against It

in excited haste, walks away from the ticket box without picking up their change. These financial perks belonged to the ticket seller.

After turning in their roll of tickets and money, most of them joined many of the other carneys at the cookhouse, for a late night sandwich or soup of the day. The cookhouse roared with laughter, loud talk and a great deal of profanity. Everyone seemed to be talking at the same time; no one cared.

Johnny thought about joining those gathered at the cookhouse but decided to remain in his trailer. He had counted the night's take and rolled all the loose change. He wasn't tired but he rarely had time to sit in quiet solitude. He relished being alone.

For a brief time last year, he had lived with a good-looking woman. She had been a sweet distraction. A mountain of problems surfaced when she persisted in making long-term plans for both of their lives. Through it all he felt guilty and sad, mostly for her, so she moved on, disappointed but undeterred. He had, almost every week, opportunities to pick up women who would consent to stay with him. He just wasn't cut out for improprieties of this nature. He couldn't explain it, but he knew it wasn't right.

To him, marriage had to be more than just stepping over a billboard (common law marriage service.) It meant a license, a commitment of love and faithful care, provision and protection. One day, with the right woman, he'd like to raise a family. It had been done before with some measure of success and happiness. The carnival wasn't such a bad place.

The next few days passed in a flurry of activity. Saturday had arrived and it was slough (taking down the carnival) night. The tear down help had been dispersed and everyone seemed to be trying to get their vehicles down the midway at the same time.

Positioning the truck or trailer next to the ride, show or joint was extremely beneficial. No one wanted to carry the numerous, and often, heavy parts and pieces any further than they had to. The tireless efforts of the next few hours were absolutely stunning. As rapidly as the shows and rides appeared, just as quickly everything disappeared.

Some of the trucks and trailers were already pulling off the lot. Johnny hadn't made up his mind whether to leave tonight or get some rest and leave in the morning. Leaving now had its advantages, less traffic, fewer flats; the cool night air not only kept the tires cooler, it also caused the engine to run stronger, longer and with a lot less heat.

Popsicle, his agent on the cork gallery, drove his joint truck, which also pulled the trailer filled with the teddy bears and slum. "Wait until tomorrow" was always his request. Trouble was, he didn't have to pay any of the bills. No, they would leave tonight. Experience had taught him to make his own decisions, even if they weren't popular.

He turned the engine over on the Buick and immediately it came to life. He was pleased with his purchase. This model was a proven winner, bullet-proof (extremely reliable.) The dynaflo transmission was ideal for pulling a house trailer. There were more

With It—For It—and Up Against It

than just a few of them on the show. He wasn't the only one who knew the car's value.

He was glad the next spot wasn't that far. Keeping Popsicle awake and on course was always difficult. Sometimes he felt like he was already raising a child. One thing he couldn't deny, Popsicle was a loyal friend and hard worker. Occasionally he would go on a three or four day drunk, but to his credit he would stay to himself and never make any trouble. The only enemy he had was himself. What set off these abbreviated binges was a mystery to everyone, including Popsicle.

This being the fifties, for the most part, there were very few turnpikes, interstates or four lane roads. His Buick had a radio, but little else in the way of options. Traversing these narrow, two lane roads was a treacherous and time-consuming task.

Long hours on the road had taught him to roll the right side windows down to cool the inside of the car and avoid drowsiness. You could crack the left side windows, but you needed to be careful or the force of the turbulent wind would burn your eyes, impeding both your vision and comfort. The results were often red eyes and a runny nose, neither of which is very pleasant.

The weight of the trailer tongue on the Buick bumper had elevated the headlights to a less than ideal height. You could easily locate squirrels in the treetops. He could never remember to adjust them. Aggravated at his unsafe procrastination, he almost missed seeing the disabled vehicle parked on the side of the road.

With It—For It—and Up Against It

He quickly stepped on the foot brake and pulled on the trailer brake handle at the same time. Making sure he was safely off the road he walked back to help the stranded motorist.

He recognized the custard (cold ice cream-like concoction usually made with pineapple flavors) truck and trailer belonging to the Browns. "Well, Johnny! I sure didn't get very far. It acts like the fuel pump has quit working," Don Brown said seriously, as he stepped down from the truck bumper.

"How about letting me take a look?" Johnny asked pleasantly, as he looked under the hood. "Where is your sediment bowl? Sometimes you can get trash in your tank and it will act just like a bad pump."

Up until then, he hadn't noticed Don's only daughter standing just out of the headlights. "Hello, Johnny! I haven't seen you in quite awhile." Her voice, rich with southern intonation, poured over him like hot oil, soothing and scintillating.

Johnny turned and realized he was looking at Pumpkin Brown and the looking wasn't bad, not bad at all. He couldn't remember the last time he had seen her. One thing was for sure, she had grown up. That was obvious.

"Why, hello Pumpkin. Your Daddy didn't tell me you were anywhere in the country." Johnny forced himself to continue searching for the problem.

After a few minutes, Johnny exclaimed, "I think I've found the problem. The sediment bowl is full of trash."

With It—For It—and Up Against It

He turned to locate a grease rag Don had placed on the fender and saw Popsicle approaching. "I didn't know if you stopped or not."

Popsicle squinted through his thick-lensed glasses and said, "You know me boss, I'm always around."

"Go turn those headlights on park before the battery goes dead," Johnny instructed. He laid a flashlight on the fender of the truck and proceeded to replace the sediment bowl. "I hope this solves our problem. Start her up Don. Let's see if we rubbed her in the right place."

The engine turned and turned until the gas finally reached the carburetor, then roared to life as Don celebrated with a Cajun yell. "Ain't that a blessing!" he exclaimed. "The Lord takes such good care of us." Johnny grinned as he continued to clean his hands. For as long as Johnny could remember, Don was always saying things he didn't understand.

Earlier in the night, when the truck broke down, Don instructed his wife and 17-year-old son to go on ahead and stop at the first truck stop. If he hadn't arrived in an hour, they were to bring back a mechanic. Not wanting to meet them returning, he quickly climbed into the truck and promised, "Follow me to the next truck stop Johnny, and I'll buy you the best steak they have."

"That's the best offer I've had all night." Johnny walked toward the car thinking, the steak might be tough, but the company will be nice.

The truck stop was buzzing with activity, the cafe was full and there were only a few choices for seating. Never one to waste an opportunity to use

With It—For It—and Up Against It

his charm, Johnny smiled at the waitress and the sea parted. "Sir, you and your party walk this way," she instructed, as she opened up the banquet room.

Johnny took his seat and noticed Pumpkin had managed to find a chair next to his, which sure didn't make him mad. After passing pleasantries with Don's wife, Silvia, and their son, Dallas, he turned his attention toward Pumpkin.

He was pleased to see the delightful signs of youthful innocence framed in her lovely face. She had a self-assured manner that enhanced her quiet demeanor.

He noticed that her hands were tanned and smooth. There were no long painted claws to impede the pursuit of purposeful living. This was a woman who embraced life, and she would never be a spectator. Life was meant to be lived. To her credit, she had made the most of what God had given her, and God had been more than generous.

"Well, what do you think?" inquired Pumpkin. "You've had a rather lengthy look."

It was then that he realized he'd been staring at her. "You left a caterpillar and came back a butterfly," he replied. "Now that takes some getting used to." He could have never imagined that little bundle of flesh and bones would turn in into this statuesque work of sculptured art.

It was good to be with his friends, enjoying good food and good conversation.

"Johnny, did you know Pumpkin finished college?" asked Silvia. "She graduated at the top of her class."

Not wanting to be the center of attention, Pumpkin laughingly stated "Small class, small college."

Johnny liked the fact that she was intelligent. What he lacked in formal education, he more than made up for in his private pursuit of knowledge. Books and the keen observations of great men and their methods had embroidered his life with treasured thoughts and ideals too numerous to name.

The steak had been to his liking, thick and juicy, the service first class. Johnny set his coffee cup down on a very generous tip. It was time to get moving; tomorrow was already here.

CHAPTER 2

The weeks passed in rapid succession. It didn't seem possible that the fair season had commenced and today was the 4th of July. The weather was unusually pleasant. The cool temperature had a positive effect on the crowd and the midway was packed. Over the years this spot had been especially good for the food concessions. There were long lines at every location. These folks loved to eat!

Johnny had thought about acquiring a couple of hot dog joints to set up in the back of the midway. There was a lot of action around the rides and there was also the advantage of selling the blow off from the girl show. (This meant the girls would conclude their performances and turn their audience out on the midway. There would be at least five hundred to a thousand potential customers walking right by a well located food joint.) To his knowledge no one had obtained an X on the back end. (No one had obtained exclusive rights to sell hot dogs in this specified

With It—For It—and Up Against It

area.) He also knew if he didn't sew it up, someone else would.

Since he had hired enough help, he was now free to keep a critical eye on his concessions. He was standing to one side of the six cat while one of his agents was working a mark.

The other agents were endeavoring to call in the passing crowd. "How about you, Lucky? Come on in and win a big one! Hey Daddy! Ho Daddy! Did you get the free one? Hey Daddy! When you came through the front gate, did you get your ticket?" What the mark did not know was there was no ticket. These tactics never failed to snare some unsuspecting person.

A large, successful looking man stepped up to the high counter to investigate the matter of a free ticket; the agent began his spellbinding enticements. From time to time the agents would throw a few pieces of stock. This subtle act of generosity always increased the size of the tip. Many onlookers became confident they could win as well.

The large man at the end of the counter was a player. He had quite a bankroll, but it was dwindling fast. He was convinced he was smarter than this lowly carnival agent. He knew some of the other players had won, he'd seen them. What he didn't know, winning and losing was at the discretion of the agent. It had nothing to do with his ability to play the game. Angry, frustrated and embarrassed at the loss of his money, the big mark realized he was busted, and he wasn't happy.

Johnny watched him with a practiced eye. There was gonna be heat and a lot of it. Bennie, the roughie he recently hired, walked up and asked, "How you wanna handle it, Boss?" This was the part of the business he hated; he tried to silence his conscience but it was no good. Something within him troubled his soul.

He had a philosophy about honest men: You couldn't beat them; they wouldn't play. The big man's greed and ego had been his undoing.

"Do you know where the Patch is?" Johnny asked.

"He was in the lush wagon," Bennie replied.

"Well, you better go get him, we're gonna need him and soon."

The lush wagon (public relations trailer) was always parked on the discreet side of the office trailer. Like the office trailer, it was a "reefer," (an enclosed custom-built semi-trailer.) The furnishing was elaborate — sumptuous couches, tasteful oriental rugs, expensive mahogany paneled walls and a well stocked bar. Every bottle was the best money could buy. A huge mural had been painted on the backside of the bar. The subject was the Midnight Review's featured burlesque star — the exotic and tantalizing, "Vanilla Sugar".

The lush wagon was a favorite watering hole for the elected officials, City, County and State. A lot of deals were cut here, a lot of money changed hands. This allowed the carnival to operate unimpeded by some bothersome statute of the law, local or otherwise. There was potential for scandal if the voters ever saw their honorable servants pie-eyed and compromised. The carnival staff took extreme measures to insure that didn't happened.

With It—For It—and Up Against It

Noble Fairly, known within the operation as the Patch – the front man for the carnival — was that insurance. With diplomatic dexterity, this charismatic public relations expert exuded hospitality and good will. He was a most proficient persuader, deal maker and all around man about town. Who knew what heights he may have risen to had he not been disbarred from a very prestigious law firm a few years ago? As Patch, his earnings were in the $200,000 range, and he was worth every penny they paid him, even though he was without certification from the State.

Johnny's roughie, Bennie, walked in the side door of the lush wagon. The refrigerated air fell on him like a cool breeze on a hot night. He stood motionless, allowing his eyes to adjust to the interior of the dimly lit bar. A number of well-dressed men were sprawled on imported leather couches.

Attending these dignitaries of prominence and power was a ramrod straight, ageless black man with a full head of gray hair. He was dressed in a dazzling white coat and dark trousers. "The ladies of the evening are never here on time," he mumbled to himself. "These political plow boys are getting restless. Some of them are way past being drunk." He was tired and ready to get out of this three-ring circus. It was the same every week, only the faces were different.

Noble Fairly was seated at the bar. As to his condition, you couldn't tell whether he'd had one drink or ten. His capacity for liquor was legendary. Always attired in the finest clothes, exotic shoes and an ostentatious diamond, he epitomized wealth and decadent living.

He was tall and wide with an imposing air that never failed to place him in an advantageous position. He was strength personified. The word was he was the prodigal son of a very prominent family back east. His lineage revealed a number of senators and one or two governors in the family tree.

"What's the story?" Noble asked, as Bennie sat down on one of the padded bar stools.

Bennie grinned. "We gotta beef down at the six cat. Looks like we're gonna need your charming intervention."

Noble sighed heavily. "That's what keeps Momma in furs," he declared, as they got up from their barstools and headed toward the midway.

Arriving on the far side of the six cat, they found Johnny trying to calm down the angry mark. Red faced and breathing heavily, it was obvious this big fella was accustomed to having his way. Trouble was, he wasn't trying to dominate one of his lodge hall buddies. He was in danger, and he didn't even know it. Benny was surprised Johnny hadn't already clipped him. He had little mercy for the large and loud. This mark was large, loud and lucky.

With practiced modulation Noble asked, "Friend, what's the trouble?" His voice, soothing and calm, smooth as velvet, arrested the ear of the agitated victim.

"I'll tell you what the trouble is," the mark replied. "This guy is a crook. Come to think about it, who are you and what business is it of yours?" he demanded, in a loud shaky voice.

With It—For It—and Up Against It

Noble stepped in closer. "There's no need to get nasty, friend. I'm on your side. To answer your question, I'm the person who's going to provide a solution to your problem." Then with a penetrating icy stare, his voice soft but now menacing, exhibiting a full measure of authority, "I'm also trying to keep you from leaving here in an ambulance. It's up to you."

The big mark was stunned. He had never been spoken to in this manner. He could well afford to lose the money, but how could he extract himself from this dilemma without sacrificing his dignity and pride? His blustery manner had always gotten him his way in times past. These carneys were unaffected by his belligerent behavior. They showed no signs of being frightened or intimidated. Who knew people could be so different? I'm calling the cops," he threatened.

"I've already sent for them," Noble replied. "Here's a thought: I'm prepared to provide you with packets of free passes for all the rides and shows, enough for you and your friends. Not only that," Noble paused and then said as a gesture of goodwill, "I'm going to allow you to select a prize of your choice. It's yours for the asking. There will be no refund. You played, you lost." He continued, "What I will do is accompany you and your friends to the grandstand ticket office. Upon arrival, I'll arrange for your entire group to attend tonight's spectacular show, Holiday On Ice, at our expense," Noble concluded, and looked directly at the surly screamer.

By now the big mark was looking for a face-saving way out and Noble had provided one. He jumped at the opportunity and said, "Friends, the pursuit of peace is of greater value than my disputed losses. Because of my forgiving nature, you're about to have the time of your life and it's not gonna cost you one thin dime," he bragged as they followed Noble Fairly down the midway.

"It almost makes you wish we'd all been robbed," whispered one of his friends, trying to keep a straight face.

Johnny was angry that the agent had busted the mark. All the old hands knew, you always let the sucker up right before he squeals; it was just good business. He decided to let the offending agent continue to work the rest of the night. He was in no mood to explain to him the rules of "fading the heat," which was nothing more than good judgement. Allowing the mark to save face by letting him win an appropriate prize, usually quelled his anger.

A cup of coffee would be good about now, Johnny thought as he moved toward the cookhouse. The fry cook was grilling onions on one side of the flattop griddle. The aroma wafted out in the midway, stirring the hunger pangs of the passers-by. It wasn't subtle, but it was very effective. Like everyone else, he had a story. He had attended culinary school and had at one time been a successful restaurateur. For whatever reason, he had climbed down into the bottom of a wine bottle and was unwilling or unable to extricate himself.

There he stood, working the front of Charity's cookhouse; an ever-present toothpick in his mouth and a pack of Lucky's rolled up in the sleeve of his

T-shirt. "What'll you have, Johnny?" he mumbled, as he turned a large mound of onions.

"Coffee, hot and black."

"Want some company?" Don Brown asked, as he sat down next to Johnny. Once again he was reminded of the strange mannerisms of Don: Carneys sat down, they didn't ask permission. It would never occur to them that someone might want to be left alone. Equally true, they didn't care!

There were other things about Don and his family that puzzled him. He'd never heard him utter one foul word, not one. He'd never seen him angry or upset. Even more perplexing, they attended church on Sunday, as often as was possible.

Last summer, Silvia had conducted some kind of a gathering called Vacation Bible School. It had been attended by most of the carney kids. Everyone said the children had a great time. Some of the parents said it was good for them. It wouldn't hurt if everyone had attended, he reasoned, then wondered where these peculiar thoughts were coming from. What did he know about Bible school?

Don laughingly observed, "I noticed you had a little run-in down at the six cat. The good thing about selling custard is, if they are unhappy with the product, they just throw it on the ground." Don reflected for a moment and remarked, "You would think they would take into account my ruffled feelings. After all, I make the wonderful stuff, but they never do, they just throw it down."

Barely listening and lost in thought, Johnny felt uneasy as he reflected on the events of the night.

With It—For It—and Up Against It

He was mystified that he hadn't cracked that smart-mouthed mark on the side of his head. He sure asked for it. Maybe he was getting soft. One thing he was sure of, it had nothing to do with being frightened or afraid. "I better get back to business or I won't have any thing to get back to," Johnny declared, as he said goodbye to Don and headed back to the six cat.

Inside his house trailer, Pollock searched around in his pockets for a match. Cupping his hand around the flame, he lit a Chesterfield and leaned back in his chair. Smoke spiraled up toward the ceiling, lazy and cordial. His night's encounter with Dixie Wright had been more than he had anticipated. He could little afford to be careless. Malcolm Wright wasn't a coward and he certainly wasn't a fool. In fact, Malcolm was cunning and extremely dangerous. Even though he was slight of stature, he was powerful in other ways. He had options others didn't have. He was connected to the bent-nosed boys in Chicago. Pollock and a few others were the only ones who knew about Malcolm's strong-armed friends. Pollock had no ambition to wind up sleeping with the fish, besides he liked his job. He enjoyed the challenge of overseeing the operation of America's largest motorized show.

As for Dixie, she was getting to be a handful. If he had it to do over, he would never have gotten involved with her. She was trouble with a capital T. He was beginning to wonder where her impetuous recklessness would take them. She had a way with him — he couldn't explain it. She was imbedded in his brain, a voluptuous nightmare, frightening and intoxicating. He was a fool, and he knew it. He was only a distraction. When she tired of him, she'd cast him off like a bad habit, but until then, all bets were off.

The remaining hours of the evening passed without further incident. Checking the callboard before going to his trailer, Johnny was pleased to see Pumpkin walking toward him. They hadn't seen each other since that night at the truck stop. Why that was, he really didn't know.

"I don't suppose you would consider buying a girl a bowl of chili," she said with a playful tone in her voice.

"Just chili?" he asked with a warm smile crinkling the lines in his face. "Does that mean you'll be paying for your own drink?"

Her eyes danced mischievously. "I guess you forgot that night my silver haired old daddy fed you a big ole steak." Waving her hands in an expansive gesture, she declared, "I want the full treatment, crackers and all the trimmings. It's not every day you get to enjoy my company. Don't you remember what my momma told you?" With a pretended dignified expression, she stated, "I graduated college, 'Chili Come Quickly'."

They decided on a food booth under the grandstand. It was quieter than the cookhouse and was operated by a group from the local Methodist Church. This bit of information was gleaned from a prominently placed sign that also served as a menu. The chili was from a can, so they settled on homemade stew.

A frail looking lady with a heavyweight smile placed the steaming bowls of stew on their table and glided away. They were delighted to discover it came with a large wedge of cornbread, precariously perched on a paper plate, with an accompanying pile of rich yellow butter.

"I'll trade you a pony ride for your cornbread," Pumpkin quipped, as she savored her first bite. "How good can you set a saddle? Do you have any boots?"

Johnny buttered a portion of the golden brown cornbread and joined in her lighthearted mood. "Don't you think that's too wild for a timid tender foot like me? Besides, I like this cornbread and I plan on eating every crumb," he said with a wave of his knife.

As they walked back to Pumpkin's trailer, little was said in the way of conversation. It had been an enjoyable encounter. Pumpkin broke the silence by inquiring, "Johnny, have you ever given any thought to settling down, getting off the road, seeing how the other half lives?"

Immediately he felt a shortness of breath. His heart was hammering louder than a cheap pocket watch. How could she possibly know what he'd been thinking? This whole night had been filled with unusual occurrences. He didn't understand his own reactions earlier in the night and now he was completely dumbfounded.

Apprehensive that she may have intruded too far into the private thoughts of this enigmatic man, Pumpkin quickly changed the subject. It was more than apparent, if there was a moment, it was now lost.

He wanted to be open and honest with her. It was important to him, but he didn't know how. He had more than just a passing interest in furthering their friendship. Abruptly he said, "You know what they say, early to bed and all that stuff. Next time, it's your turn to feed me." He wanted to stay but felt compelled to leave. She was so beautiful and unpretentious. Why did he have this unexplainable urge to flee? How did his life get so complicated after one bowl of stew?

After Johnny left, Pumpkin sat on the trailer steps and pondered the unsettlingly moments of the last few minutes. She remembered how she felt when she saw him that night on the side of the road, his head peering under the hood of her daddy's truck. She was smitten! She knew it was impulsive, she knew it was impetuous, and she also knew it was more than an infatuation.

Long ago she had committed her life to Jesus Christ. In recent years, she had petitioned the Lord to direct her steps regarding a husband. She was certain Johnny Palmer was God's gift to her.

Religion would recite his reckless lifestyle, his sin and his shortcomings. Redemption would rescue him and unite him with the God of all creation. Pumpkin wasn't religious, so there was no hesitation. She saw him not as he was, but as he would be; forgiven, changed, reborn and living his life for Jesus.

CHAPTER 3

꧁ ꧂

Claude Brimbly was up on the bally platform, prowling like a big cat, back and forth with energetic expectation as he worked the crowd. He was good, he knew he was good. He'd been at it long enough. He barked out his rhythmic call, "Hey, Hi, Look! It's gonna be all free down here at the circus side show. Freaks, curiosities, oddities of all kinds, alive and on the inside. Step in closer folks. Don't block the midway. You won't believe your eyes! I'm about to bring on stage every mother's nightmare — 'Billy the frog boy'! My God, how does he live?" The crowd pushed in toward the platform for a closer look, their faces now fashioned with expectation and apprehension.

Billy the frog boy's tiny body was hidden in a white laundry bag that had been placed in a large galvanized wash tub. There was a runway built especially for his entrance. The tub was placed inside the runway and pushed onto the stage. The

With It—For It—and Up Against It

most rewarding part of this theatrical presentation was that magical moment when Claude thrust the microphone down in the wash tub. The inquisitive interest of the audience was fanned into flames by the shrill mumbling of Billy's voice. The crowd couldn't get to the ticket box fast enough. Claude watched the tent fill up with paying customers. 'I love my job,' he thought, 'working these State Fairs makes it even better.'

Across the fairgrounds, many visitors were looking through the livestock barns. They were full of the various breeds of cattle, hogs, sheep and other types of animals.

This was the big show — the State Fair. Expectations were high. Exhibit buildings were filled with crafts, canning and cookery. The contestants were a hodge-podge of men, women and children all with one dream — the grand prize.

Silvia and Pumpkin enjoyed getting away from the midway, if only for a little while. The exhibit hall was overflowing with all kinds of homemade quilts, tablecloths and other wonderful demonstrations of artistic creativity.

These were the good ol' days. People took pride in their products, it didn't matter whether they were manufactured in Maine or came out of the ground in Georgia. America's productivity and ingenuity was supreme throughout the world; 'Made in Japan' was as close to cussing as you could get. There was an innocence and independence that prevailed in the land. American factories and farms were supplying the entire world with goods and services. There was

With It—For It—and Up Against It

a willingness to work, to sacrifice, and to succeed. Fiercely competitive, the folks of the red, white and blue daily proved their superior skills and craftsmanship. It was easy to see why it was marked, 'Made in America.' It ain't bragging, if you can back it up.

Silva and Pumpkin were surprised to see Dixie strolling down one of the other aisles. As yet, she had not noticed them.

Bored and restless, Dixie had ambled into the exhibit hall quite by accident. She had little use for anything homemade. Most of her youthful years had been spent in hand-me down clothes her mother had made for her older sisters. Her family had been known as poor white trash. Her daddy was a wife beater and a womanizer. There had been scores of nights she and her sisters had been victimized, physically and sexually. Little was known in those days about what went on inside the Ballard's house.

One night, her father in a drunken rage, busted and broke almost everything in the house. Dixie lay in her narrow bed trembling, frightened and afraid. Tonight was different from all the other nights of terror; she had a plan. She had decided she was going to end this ungodly assault on her sisters and herself. Tucked under her pillow was a loaded 22 caliber revolver, and she knew how to use it.

Dixie watched as her father's silhouette filled the doorframe. Her hands were shaking violently as she pointed the gun in his direction. His face curled in a sadistic sneer. "What do you think you're gonna do with that pea shooter?" She knew if she waited, she would lose any advantage she had. The roar of the gun seemed unusually loud. There was screaming and wailing; she thought it was her sisters. Unaware of her own screaming, she held on to the trigger until the gun clicked its statement of impotence.

Her father's face, revealing shock and unbelief, seemed to sag in unison with his body as he fell to the floor. The irregular pattern of bullet holes was seeping blood from the side of his face all the way down his right thigh. "You've done it girl. You've killed me," he stated, in a matter of a fact way.

Dixie placed her meager belongings in a brown paper bag and ran out the door. Unable to stop crying, she headed toward the highway. She could hardly believe what had happened. There was no regret. She had intended to shoot him. God knows he deserved it. What she couldn't fathom was her inability to regain her composure. She hadn't considered what she would do after she shot him. Even now it seemed like a bad dream. The roar of a passing truck, too close for comfort, awakened her. It was then she realized she was running down the middle of the highway.

The big truck's air brakes hissed in violent protest, as the driver brought the west coast B model Mack to a stop. The trucker opened the door and walked around in front of the headlights. "Little lady, are you alright?" inquired the tired looking man.

Ignoring his question she asked, "Where are you headed?"

"I'm unloading in Las Vegas in three days if I'm lucky."

"What about taking me with you?"

With It—For It—and Up Against It

"Are you in some kind of trouble?" he questioned, as he looked at her makeshift luggage.

"Yes, but it needn't concern you, I promise I won't be any trouble." "How about it? Be a sport. Can I go with you?"

He was real sleepy and he wouldn't mind some company, plus he was the kind of man that enjoyed helping people. It was more than obvious this girl needed help. "Why not! Climb up in there. Let's get rolling."

Dixie placed her sack of clothes in the spacious sleeper compartment behind the seat and settled in for the ride. The night's tragedy grew dimmer with each passing mile. Who knew what tomorrow would bring? It would have to be better than today.

The Mack engine was purring like a neutered tomcat. The driver, inspired that he had an audience, was working the two sticks on those triplex transmissions like a man possessed. He was making time and the scenery inside the cab was easy on the eye. With her on board, Las Vegas didn't seem that far.

Dixie stood in the exhibition hall frozen in thought, reliving her tormented past.

Silvia turned around and made her way toward the front of the exhibit building. Pumpkin had left a short time ago. Lately, she seemed preoccupied. Silvia had attempted to uncover the reasons for her silent moments of distracted thought. Pumpkin had passed it off a little too nonchalantly and hurried back to the custard joint.

It was then, Sylvia spotted Dixie again, standing transfixed. This would be an excellent opportunity to

With It—For It—and Up Against It

strike up a conversation. Who knows what the Lord may do, she thought, as she hurried up to Dixie?

"Why Silvia, where did you come from?" Dixie asked, as she came back to reality. She liked Silvia from the moment they had been introduced. They hadn't spent much time together these past few years for reasons unknown to both of them.

Silvia had an elegance and charm that Dixie admired. There was in her countenance a radiance that was inexplicable. Her own mother had been coarse and closed-mouthed. She knew nothing of God and His plan for her life or her daughters. Dixie was an example of a child raised in a godless home.

"I noticed you and your family were all dressed up Sunday morning." Dixie observed.

"I'm glad you noticed. We were headed for church. The next time we get a chance to go I'll let you know, maybe you'll come with us."

The look on Dixie's face betrayed her thoughts; 'it's not likely.' The only thing she knew about church was what she'd seen in Arnold Blackwood's ding show. A ding show was a tent, or more often a trailer, where the public was invited to enter without paying an admission charge. After they viewed the contents inside they were then ushered by a most persuasive attendant who would require of them a substantial donation before exiting.

Blackwood had framed his ding show within the confines of a beautiful 36-foot custom-built semi-trailer. On the inside was an unbelievable reproduction of Leonardo da Vinci's painting of the Lord's Last Supper. Amazingly, in grand carnival fashion, the mural was over 12 feet wide, a veritable gold mine, a stroke of genius. Appropriate music, softly played, filled the surrounding area with a religious reverence that never failed to empty the public's pocket book. Jesus fed the multitudes; Blackwood was faithfully fleecing them.

Standing in the exhibit hall with Silvia, Dixie's mind went back to that day last summer when she stood gazing at Blackwood's enlarged presentation of the Last Supper. The meaning, though veiled, was not altogether lost on her. Something within her mellowed. She felt a strange stirring. The music was enchanting, the characters intriguing. She knew little of the meaning of the story that was being portrayed. Strangely striken, she felt a kinship with the figures.

Somehow, she understood the agony they were endeavoring to bear. The fellowship of their suffering caused her pain and sadness. It was a most troubling experience. She had no intention of ever going back.

Her thoughts were interrupted by the approach of Malcolm's office flunky, Shorty Yeager. "Malcolm is looking for you. I think he wants to take you to lunch."

Dixie didn't like Shorty, he was a snitch, and his main project was spying on her and she knew it. Without a word to him, she said goodbye to Silvia, and headed toward the office.

Malcolm sank down in the huge leather office chair; it had been his dad's. The massive desk, the dated furnishings were all just as they had been when his father ran the Show. He missed his father. He'd

With It—For It—and Up Against It

died just as he'd lived, on the midway, taking care of business.

Through his tireless efforts, The Mighty Wright Shows had become the largest motorized carnival in America. There was only one other Show bigger than theirs was, and that Show traveled on a train.

Lately, the competition had been annoying and frustrating. The fair committees were becoming impossible to deal with, loyalty and integrity sadly lacking in their character. Their only interest is money and how much they can get, he thought, as his mood darkened with each passing minute. They didn't seem to understand that the carnival world had a code of conduct, a way of doing business, and loyalty was the chief cornerstone of that code.

In the old days, everything was done on a handshake. If a man's word wasn't any good, writing it down on paper certainly wouldn't help.

Last fall he'd lost a big fair over some made up technicality. A bushel basket full of lawyers and a pickup load of signed contracts had absolutely no effect on the outcome. It wasn't that he was outclassed. In fact, the other carnival wasn't as large or as well run. He lost the fair because of unethical business practices, perpetrated by some Johnny-come-lately Show owner. That was a matter yet to be settled. Acts of conspiracy would not be tolerated.

There were other problems. The carnival business was beginning to feel the impact of air conditioners and television. The influence of these modern appliances was becoming more wide spread with the passing of each new day. If the last two years was any indication, change was already coming, and fast cutting into the profits.

The fair was a gigantic event. In the past, people waited all year to celebrate and spend their money. They were accustomed to the heat, which seldom hindered their attendance during the day. They hadn't become shackled to their TV and its expanding programs. Consequently, they were attending the carnival at night. Carnivals had all day and night to do business — to make money. Today, people were staying at home out of the heat watching TV. These modern conveniences were impacting show business with dwindling hours and diminishing returns.

As Malcolm thought about these challenges, memories of his early years with Dixie surfaced. It had been a while since he'd given any thought to their wild and irresponsible first encounter.

Las Vegas was the site of their whirlwind courtship, if you could call it that. He was in town on business — negotiations had stalled and the parties involved had become ineffectual. It was agreed that the meeting would be adjourned until the following day, allowing every one time to cool off.

He had left the hotel and decided a brisk walk would relieve the tension of the meeting. He hadn't gone three steps when his eyes fell on Dixie. She was carrying an old brown paper bag. Later he learned; it contained everything she had in the world.

At first, he couldn't figure out why he was so infatuated by her. She was rumpled and wrinkled. Her hair was stringy and she definitely needed a bath. There was something about the way she carried herself. Her body language was both docile and defiant. There was fire in her eyes, but there was also a vulnerability that exposed the inexperience of her youth and the fact that she was in trouble.

Upon closer observation, it became apparent she had a lot going for her. She was very well endowed, face and figure without flaw. He wondered what she would look like if the hotel staff gave her the once over, including the spa. He didn't want to appear like a lecherous old reprobate. Well, he thought, all she can do is say no.

Never known as a ladies man, Malcolm tried to hide the small tremor in his voice as he spoke to Dixie, "Please excuse my unsolicited intrusion, but you look like you could use a friend. If I'm correct, let me assure you I have no ulterior motive, I just want to help you." Malcolm looked kindly into her eyes.

Dixie looked at the well-dressed man, searching his face for a clue. Why would someone like him want to help her?

The long ride she shared with the tired-eyed trucker had been a pleasant but exhausting ordeal. At no time had she felt apprehensive or afraid; quite the opposite, as he had been kind, very respectful and generous. Her meals, snacks and any drinks had been furnished at his expense. The trucker seemed to take pleasure in providing for her.

Maybe because of his admirable behavior, she was prepared to consider this middle-aged man's offer. She needed a friend; what she didn't need was trouble. She had enough trouble, heartache and despair to last a lifetime, even though she was still a teenager. She was certain that by now the law was looking for her. In her present condition, she was about as conspicuous as a parakeet at a cockfight.

"By *helping*, you mean exactly what?"

"Well for starters a room, a bath and a hot meal. Are you interested?"

"How am I going to pay for all this luxurious living? You see what my irresistible charm has provided up until now." She managed a slight grin.

"My name is Malcolm Wright, young lady. You let me worry about the details. For now, just place yourself in my capable hands." Gesturing for her to follow, Malcolm made his way back to the hotel.

Dixie followed Malcolm into the main lobby, feeling very much out of place. It seemed like every one was starring at her. One thing did surprise her; the manager behind the reservation desk hardly lifted an eyebrow. He obviously knew her new-found benefactor. Malcolm signed the registry and held a brief conversation with the manager, who immediately began giving instructions to the Hotel staff.

"What shall I call you?" Malcolm asked, as he and Dixie walked to the elevator door.

"Dixie, Dixie Ballard." Malcolm pushed the button and waited for the elevator to appear. The ride up was smooth and quick. The operator stopped the elevator on the tenth floor. The door opened, revealing a narrow hallway leading to a select number of rooms. Malcolm walked to the appropriate numbered room, turned the key in the lock, opened the door and invited her to go in.

The inside was as spectacular as anything she'd seen in the movies or anywhere else she'd ever been. The room was enchantingly beautiful, spacious, luxurious and immaculate.

Malcolm watched as she set the brown paper bag down. Her shoulders gently shuddered as tears welled up in her eyes. "Is all this for me?"

"It is, and what's more, there is a regiment of beauticians, manicurists, masseurs and a collection of clothing headed your way." "I have also arranged for room service. I wasn't sure what you liked. They suggested an assortment of delicacies. I trust you'll find something to your liking." He watched Dixie roaming through the rooms as innocent as a child. "You are going to be occupied for the next few hours and I have a few phone calls to make. What about dinner? Think you might be ready to eat about eight?"

"If this isn't a dream I will." Dixie swirled around the room.

Back in his hotel room, Malcolm reflected on the events of the day. He thought about calling his father, but he really didn't have any news. Dad was probably so involved with all the work in winter quarters he didn't have time for idle chitchat. Malcolm was seldom alone by choice. The death of his wife seven years ago had left him lonely and ill at ease. She'd died in an automobile accident. There were no children. His wife had been unable to have any. They'd talked about adoption, but somehow they never got around to doing it. He missed her. She had been a faithful friend and wife. He'd never gotten used to life without her.

Suddenly without reason, he felt tired and old. Drawing the drapes, he decided a nap was just what he needed. The dinner date with Dixie had him feeling anxious and excited. It had been a long time since he'd had feeling of any kind; maybe he wasn't over the hill after all.

At eight o'clock, Malcolm returned to Dixie's hotel room and knocked softly on the oak finished door. In a matter of moments, the door swung open and there stood Dixie. He could barely believe his eyes. She looked fantastic. She was wearing a sophisticated evening dress, simple and black. It adorned her body in sensual elegance, far greater than the designer dared hope for or imagined. Her face was aglow with youthful exuberance, her bare shoulders creamy and soft. Her toes, painted and small, were peeking out of a pair of expensive, open-toed shoes with high heels.

She looked like a fashion model off the cover of *Vogue*. Her dark hair was rich and full, her mouth luscious red and inviting. As Malcolm feasted his eyes upon her, he realized he felt twenty years younger. Tonight was going to be special.

CHAPTER 4

Pete made his way down the midway with a shuffling tenacity; his disfigured limbs a testimony of the unavoidable wages that danger earns. In his youth he had embraced the bar of the high trapeze. His enduring love affair with lady luck had clouded his judgement and ended his legendary career. Fallen and crumpled in a mangled heap beneath his exalted empire, he was cast down, to rule no more.

Johnny was sitting on the high counter of the six cat as Pete approached. "This midway gets longer every week." Pete sighed and mopped sweat from his brow.

Johnny liked to aggravate the old man. "You are just getting old and contrary." Everyone knew Pete was always positive and full of amusing stories. He delighted in making people laugh. If he'd ever had a troubled thought, you'd never know it.

"Careful now, I'm here on official business. Malcolm asked me to come by and invite you to a little shindig at the lush wagon tomorrow night after the show closes," Pete said with exaggerated importance.

"What's the deal, Pete?"

"It's a celebration my boy, a tribute to justice. It's taken place on this exact date every year for the last four years. Not many people are invited and even less know why they have been invited."

"Put my name in that category. I don't have a clue. There's a story here somewhere and you know all about it. Do you have time to tell the it or would you rather I remained both ignorant and ugly?"

Where do I start and what can I say, Pete wondered as he thoughtfully rubbed his chin, remembering that about four months after Malcolm and Dixie were married the truth came out. Dixie was arrested and taken back to her hometown in Georgia. The charge was attempted murder, unlawful flight and a number of other indictments.

Her father had survived the shooting but the multiple gunshot wounds had left him crippled in mind and body. He barely knew his own name. Confined to a wheel chair, he was living in a nursing home on the outskirts of town. For the first time in their sad lives, Dixie's mother and sisters were living without fear or torment. Their days of being savaged were over. Dixie had made sure of that.

The details of the trial became front-page news. Reporters came from as far away as Atlanta. Arriving from New York City, the highly prized defense attorney, Noble Fairly served as Dixie's counsel.

With It — For It — and Up Against It

The attorney for the prosecution was a sympathetic drinking buddy of Dixie's father, an unconscionable man named Eli Wall. He was a deceitful man with ambitious goals and little ability, a small town lawyer with an even smaller grasp of the ethics of law.

Standing in front of the jury and pointing his finger at Dixie, Eli said, in a voice brimming with condemnation, "She's a tramp, a child of malevolent hatred who shot her daddy in cold blood as easily as she would have pulled a weed out of a flower bed — a promiscuous premeditated murderer whose only regret was her failure to end her father's life."

Prejudicial witnesses had come forward spewing out imaginary tales filthy enough to have been birthed in the vilest brothel in Sodom and Gomorrah. The jury didn't believe it; neither did anyone else, except Malcolm. Being a prideful man, he felt embarrassed and ashamed. He had been stunned at the licentious attack of the prosecution. At a time when Dixie desperately needed him, he was lost in his own world of self-pity and loathing.

With poise and skill, Dixie's defense attorney Noble Fairly stood and began to weave, with meticulous care, the events leading up to that fateful night. With quiet dignity, he exposed the courtroom to the encompassing destruction of rape and sexual battery, the madness it brings to the innocent minds of the abused. Then with a flourish of flamboyance, he riveted the jury to the edge of their seats when he roared with indignation; "anyone would have done what Dixie did, only a lot sooner."

It was no contest; the good people of the state of Georgia were outraged at the beastly behavior of Dixie's black-hearted father. In less time than it takes to play a good game of pool, the jury returned with the verdict: Not Guilty!

The condensed narrative of Dixie's trial spilled out of Pete's mouth in an unfamiliar monotone. The eyes of the old showman became dull and lifeless. The pain and sadness that had pierced his tough exterior announced its presence in his parting words: "Dixie was never the same after that damn trial. Neither was Malcolm, come to think about it."

Johnny sat there wondering about what he had just seen and heard. He would later learn that years ago Malcolm's father, J. D. Wright, had helped Pete financially. After the trapeze accident in the circus Big Top, J. D. was instrumental in aiding and assisting Pete's move from the circus into the carnival business. Pete never forgot J. D.'s kindness, and to this day, he was the Wright family's most loyal supporter and friend.

The next day passed in a blur. After the show closed, it was time to make an appearance at the Wright's traditional private get-together. Johnny climbed the steps to the side entrance of the lush wagon, wondering what to expect. He wasn't much of a party animal, preferring the solitude of a good book and a Cuban cigar.

The party was in full swing. The room was pulsating with an excited effervescence. There were only a handful of partygoers, but that's all it takes. Carneys are notoriously wild and uninhibited. The festivities were definitely exclusive. With the exception of Noble Fairly, none of the carnival staff had been invited.

Finding plenty of space at the bar, Johnny sat down on a padded stool, delighted to discover Pete was tending bar.

"What will it be, Sonny?" Pete asked with a big grin.

"A splash of Crown Royal wouldn't make me mad. How did you wind up with this job? You know they'll be cussing you before the night's over." Johnny looked around the room.

"I'm a public-minded citizen. I felt it was my duty to irritate and annoy this bunch of plunderers." Pete laughed heartily and poured Johnny a water glass more than half full of Crown Royal.

Johnny looked at the glass of whiskey and said, "If I didn't know better I'd think you were trying to get me drunk and take advantage of me."

Pete heard little of Johnny's last remarks. Loud requests from the other end of the bar required his attention.

"Pour it slow till I say, 'woah'," instructed one of the men at the bar.

"You got it, that's why they pay me the big bucks."

Dixie was pleased when she noticed Johnny at the bar. She hated hosting this party and was certain Malcolm had been repeating this tired celebration out of spite. The trial had taken something out of both of them. She wanted to forget, to move on, to stop rehearsing the grizzly details. Four years was enough.

She wanted her life back. She wanted Malcolm back. The odds of that happening were depressingly remote. The kind, attentive man she met in Las Vegas had disappeared in a bottle of gin.

If only J. D. were alive. He had been her most faithful supporter and friend. From the moment Malcolm had introduced them, he immediately embraced her as a daughter. It was love at first hug. He was a grand old man who saw the good in everyone.

Their gratifying relationship was short-lived. J. D. died six months after the trial. After the funeral, Malcolm forfeited all claims to happiness, plunging downward into a self-imposed exile. He began to drink heavily and took little notice of Dixie. What he did see, he didn't care for because to him she was damaged goods. The wickedness of those lying witnesses had settled in his soul. He became bitter and short-tempered, impossible to live with.

Dixie knew what she had become, but she didn't care. If her husband didn't want her, she would find someone who did. With her dark smoldering good looks, attracting men had been easy. When she tired of the affair, getting rid of them had been the problem. The latest puppet she'd put on a string was going to be a lot more difficult to get rid of. She was already tired of Pollock. His juvenile advances had become a nuisance. He had become jealous and possessive, always inquiring after her whereabouts. Needy and weak, she couldn't stand for him to touch her anymore. It was over, but she knew she had to be careful. He was a dangerous man, accustomed to having his way.

Turning her attention toward the bar, Dixie decided she needed a refill and headed toward Johnny. "Buy a girl a drink?" She sat down next to him.

"How about I give you part of mine?" Johnny stated in a good-natured way. "Pete emptied a pint of whiskey in this water glass. He's real generous with your liquor."

Dixie looked seductively into his eyes and teasingly replied, "Maybe he's intending to steal your bankroll after you pass out. He's an unscrupulous old codger."

Dixie was glad that Johnny had come to the party. Here's a man she had been unable to attract. It was almost like a challenge. Always polite, always the gentleman, he never gave any indication he was interested in her. She was intrigued with his aloof manner. He was friendly, but only up to a point. It wasn't just her. He was that way with everybody, that is, everybody except Pumpkin Brown.

Knowing the Brown's pursuit of moral excellence, Dixie hadn't invited them. She decided this party atmosphere would offend their Christian values. It also allowed her the opportunity to gain the full attention of Johnny. Without Pumpkin's presence, she could handle any other distractions that might arise.

Johnny was enjoying the conversation; it was light and familiar. Dixie was easy to be with. Her laughter came out soft and throaty, almost smoky. She smelled wonderful! When she leaned forward he could feel her breath on his neck. It was a tantalizing distraction.

The bar light shimmered over her body caressing every curve. She was a knockout; there's no denying that. He knew his feelings were inappropriate. Maybe it was the whiskey. Maybe it was her. All he knew was he was enjoying himself. The drinks kept coming and they continued getting to know each other, better and better.

The articulate voice of Noble Fairly cut through their flirtatious small talk. "Do you realize the company you're keeping?"

Dixie gave Johnny a playful nudge. "Which one of us are you referring to?"

Noble looked amused. "Whichever one of you designated Pete as bartender, that 's a criminal act in and of itself." Noble pointed around the room. "The show won't open on time tomorrow if it's up to this bunch of drunks."

As Noble continued the conversation, Johnny's head began to clear. It was time to leave. He felt like he'd lost control of his faculties. He learned one thing tonight; Dixie Wright was a spellbinder and a mesmerizer. He was far from being what he ought to be, but he wasn't a skirt chaser and he certainly didn't mess around with another man's wife. Until tonight he'd never been tempted to go beyond his comfortably arranged convictions. Thankfully his sanity returned, and he headed for the door. He would say goodbye tomorrow, he reasoned as the cool late night air continued to clear his head.

Dixie was disappointed that her opportunity with Johnny had been interrupted. He was everything she had imagined and more. He was deceptively mascu-

With It—For It—and Up Against It

line and hard bodied. What woman wouldn't be overwhelmed with his charm? Whoever lands him will know that dreams really do come true — just not her dreams she thought, as sadness crept across her face.

The day following the party, Pumpkin was up earlier than usual. She had tossed and turned until daylight. Unable to sleep she had spent the night distressed and pouting about Johnny. His attendance at the Wright's celebration party was a troubling thorn in her thoughts. Why he'd felt obligated to go was a mystery to her. Then again, maybe he wanted to be there. These and other thoughts had evolved into agitation and depression.

Presently, she was furious with him and his idea of courtship, if that's what you call it. She realized up until now she had been dating boys, college boys, but boys nonetheless. Johnny was her first entrée into the complex world of older men.

She knew he wanted to be with her but she never saw him. He had a funny way of expressing his interest in her. If absence makes the heart grow fonder, Johnny's love and passion for her must be quite intense she decided.

She passed the early morning hours by giving attention to her hair, makeup and what to wear. She was a beautiful woman and today she was more striking than usual.

Her mother had made a few suggestions about how you get into a man's heart, none of which coincided with hers. Out of respect, Pumpkin listened, but her mind was made up, she was heading toward the cookhouse. Johnny Palmer was having company for breakfast whether he wanted it or not.

Bill Charity had just placed a triple order of ham and eggs in front of Johnny when Pumpkin walked in and sat down beside him. "What's the matter, didn't they have any more eggs?" Pumpkin asked, as she looked at Johnny's mountain of eggs and slabs of ham. Toast was piled six slices high and another plate was piled high with potatoes.

"I'd answer you, but momma told me not to talk when my mouth's full," Johnny teased as he signaled for Bill.

Pumpkin ordered coffee and dry toast. "How was the party last night? You don't look like death warmed over. You must have had sweet milk to drink and pure thoughts about everyone."

Johnny sprinkled salt on his potatoes and gave her a grin. "It was chocolate milk. After all, it was a party. In regard to my thoughts, I never reveal what I'm thinking."

With a slight tremor in her voice, Pumpkin went on the offensive. "Being the good little girl that I am, I wasn't invited." Then in a sarcastic southern tone she said, "Pa don't allow me to go nowhere until all the cows are milked."

Johnny didn't like the way Pumpkin was behaving. He had nothing to do with who the Wright's invited. He was surprised his name had been on the guest list. It was early and his head hurt. He had no idea how to placate her smoldering anger. He hadn't gone to the party with any thought of upsetting her. However, he had no intention of asking her for permission to go — not then, not now, not ever.

He knew he was not without flaws and shortcomings. He had purposely avoided Pumpkin. The reasons were simple: He was laboring to sort out his emotions, his feelings, his thinking. For the first time in his life he felt an urgency to be with someone. Pumpkin was in his thoughts constantly. He had never dealt with feelings of this kind before. All the other women he'd known, he could take or leave, it didn't matter, but with Pumpkin, it was different.

He knew she was waiting for an explanation that would satisfy her inquisitive mind. Right now, he couldn't think of anything that would reassure her. His mind was blank.

He was grateful when Agitatin' Bill plopped down on the other side of Pumpkin. "Hey, Johnny I see you're having your usual setting of eggs and hindquarter of hog." Turning to Pumpkin, he quipped, "What brings you out among the freaks and felons at such an early hour?"

Pumpkin arched an eyebrow. "I just thought I'd see how the maligned and the declined embrace the day."

She liked Agitatin' Bill. He was a hard worker and unlike some, always clean and well groomed. There was a reason for his nickname: He delighted in controversy and confrontation. He showed no favoritism. He faithfully stirred the tumultuous pot of everyone's emotions. He was good-natured about every thing, but he loved to aggravate and agitate anyone, anywhere. His most notable victim was Malcolm Wright himself. However, Malcolm's present frame of mind did not lend itself to any light-hearted amusement. Some of Agitatin' Bill's friends feared one day he might go too far.

Pumpkin suddenly realized she had made a mistake in coming to the cookhouse. This was the wrong place and the wrong time to be sifting through their inconsistent relationship. As her anger abated, she searched for a way to leave, gracefully if possible. Her father unknowingly provided her with the opportunity.

Don Brown walked into the cookhouse and up to their table, immediately sensing the tension between Johnny and Pumpkin. Not one to intrude he turned and moved toward another table. Pumpkin spoke quickly, "That's all right, Dad, you can sit here. I need to find Dallas. He wanted me to help him clean the custard stand. I'm afraid I am more than late. I'll see you back at the trailer." With a wave goodbye to Johnny, Pumpkin made a graceful exit out of the cookhouse.

Shorty Yeager was replacing burnt out light bulbs on the front gate when he noticed Pumpkin leaving the cookhouse. Shorty was a "jack of all trades." He set up and tore down, and took care of the light towers, as well as the front gate.

He also served as mailman for the carnival. This consisted of going to the main post office in each town on a regular basis and calling for the mail addressed, *In Care of the Mighty Wright Shows*. The carney's name would be addressed on the envelope or package. The second line would read, *In Care of the Mighty Wright Shows*, and then the name of the city and state.

Shorty also sold and distributed the carney bible known as, *The Billboard*. This weekly publication gave news and information relating to fairs, carnivals and amusement parks.

He was just about to call out to Pumpkin when Pollock walked up. "How was the party last night?" Shorty asked innocently.

Pollock seemed to stiffen and snort all at the same time. Shorty knew he had asked the wrong question. "Some of us have to work for a living. I haven't got time for butt kissing and cake baking," Pollock declared, as he stormed past the ladder Shorty was standing on.

I best hurry, Shorty thought; it's almost time to open.

He turned and noticed that up and down the midway awnings were being lifted, counters were being cleaned, engines on the rides were being gassed up, all in preparation for another day.

Shorty was just about to climb down the ladder when a local taxicab pulled up to the front gate. The door opened and out stepped Vanilla Sugar. She was covered from head to toe in fashionable and expensive clothing. Perched on her head was a large brimmed hat, sunglasses, and on her hands long white gloves. Every precaution possible had been taken to insure that not one ray of unwanted sunlight touched her creamy albino-like skin.

She moved with the rhythmic motion of a dancer gliding over the ground. This was no hoochey coochey momma who would take it all off for a few dollars. This was an exquisite meticulous, burlesque star, seductive and delicious. Vanilla Sugar was valued and pampered as much, or more, than a Hollywood starlet. Accompanying her down the midway was a large, well built man with searching eyes.

Noble Fairly nodded in pleasured approval as Vanilla Sugar gracefully swept by him. He had just stepped out of the office trailer en route to a new show that had joined for the next three spots. With long strides, he walked toward the backend of the midway, pleased to discover everything was first class, clean, well maintained, open and doing well.

There was the usual presentation of large canvass pictures hanging in a straight line, known in the business as a banner line. These works of the show painter's art are intended to entice people to purchase a ticket.

There was nothing extraordinary about the banners, but the bally platform was most unusual. It wasn't any taller or wider than any other show platform. The difference was, on one side of the platform beyond the ticket box a white Cadillac ambulance poked its grill out into the midway, imposing its will on the unsuspecting public.

A mournful wail loudly sounded by an amplified siren arrested the attention of everyone within hearing distance. On stage was a tall theatrical-looking senior citizen with piercing eyes and a full head of unmanageable white hair. Dressed in a three-quarter-length white laboratory coat, he looked like a mad scientist, a discredited double for Vincent Price. Noble stood transfixed as the crowd magically increased in number, pushing and shoving, trying to get as close to the platform as possible.

Dr. Dubious, with microphone in hand, began to move about the platform in an unsteady gait. His disability was not the result of some unfortunate accident in a scientific laboratory. His faltering footwork was the result of bad choices and bathtub gin.

Accompanying him on stage was a former beauty queen, tired eyed, sad-faced and way past her prime. She was attired in an extremely tight nurse's uniform that revealed a dissipated body ravaged by long hours, lost hope and hard living.

As the wailing siren subsided to a low moaning whimper with practiced timing, Dr. Dubious began his declaration of horror. "Ladies and gentlemen, beyond this banner line, behind this platform, yonder inside that formidable tent six feet beneath the earth, a brave soul has been willingly hypnotized and buried alive."

The crowd stampeded toward the ticket box to secure their passport into the land of the macabre. Noble waved at the ticket seller and followed the spellbound patrons into the tent.

On the inside, a column-shaped viewing glass rose out of the dusty earth revealing a man of average size in quiet repose within the narrow confines of a coffin buried six feet underground.

It would seem to be a peaceful arrangement. At the propitious moment, the unconscious knowledge of his ghastly surroundings motivates his hypnotized body to thrash about in ghoulish display. The buried subject is a most believable pretender.

The women screamed, the children cried, and the men turned pale; as a publicity stunt, it was priceless. The beauty of this bizarre burial is not just the initial avalanche of cash; this Professor of Pretension had devised a plan whereby he could sell these same customers another ticket. On the last night of the fair at the appointed hour, this silver haired persuader of the preposterous is going to uncover the grave and awaken his hypnotized subject.

Hundreds will circle that lowly mound of clay to witness this glorious resuscitation. Noble shook his head in amazement and walked out of the tent.

CHAPTER 5

~

Malcolm Wright was more agitated than usual. One of the most depressing places to be on a rainy day is a fairground; everything shuts down. Everyone on the midway has a reason to sing the blues.

The rain had been falling like droplets of disaster for two days. The melancholy moisture may have met the needs of the farmer and his crops, but it was a revenue-robbing distraction for the carnival.

The midway was as muddy as a Louisiana bayou. Many of the carneys had worked throughout the morning in a futile attempt to drain water off the midway. Malcolm slogged through the rain and mud in a slicker suit and overshoes. What they needed was sunshine and a lot of it. Right now, it didn't look very promising.

This was the first day in months that he had not had a drink before breakfast. His mouth was dry and he was sweating.

With It—For It—and Up Against It

To say he'd had some kind of moment, an epiphany, would not be accurate. What he had experienced was a certain knowing that he was going to lose everything his father had worked for if he didn't make some changes. The recent loss of one of their best fairs had alerted him to the warning signs.

His behavior had been less than professional. The displeased fair board had awarded the contract to another carnival. He was ashamed that he had allowed himself to become so irresponsible. He was determined to get off the booze and he was equally resolved to make peace with Dixie. Maybe there was still a chance they could save their marriage.

As Malcolm approached the entrance to the cookhouse, the lively sounds of laughter inside belied the grim atmosphere outside. The rain had sent the carneys seeking shelter and a little enjoyment. He found a chair next to Noble Fairly, who was finishing up a plate of French toast. Malcolm marveled at the man's precise mannerisms. Everything was just so. He went at his French toast like a master craftsman. Even his appearance was amazing. Somehow, Noble had managed to traverse the muddy lot without soiling his clothes or his shoes! He was immaculate. If only everything in his world was so precise! Because of the rain, neither one of them felt like talking. Coffee was ordered and little said.

Malcolm grimaced as he looked down at the coffee that had been placed before him. He didn't want it. What he wanted was a drink. His hands were shaking as he lifted the hot liquid to his mouth.

Noble noticed his boss's unsteady attempt, recognizing the symptoms he'd suffered himself more times than he cared to remember. With a subtle gesture, Noble laid his hand on Malcolm's shoulder. "Buck up bully boy, you can do it," Noble softly said, as he got up and walked out of the cookhouse.

Agitatin' Bill and his longtime friend, Snag Hughes, were wading through the mud and water on the backside of the midway. The slippery earth was a real problem for Snag. He was a large, barrel-like man. His imposing weight was making deep tracks in the mud. His hands were wide and thick, powerful beyond belief. He could easily break the handles or jaws out of the best pair of pliers that could be bought.

Thankfully, he was a gentle soul who loved stray dogs and little children. In the next few moments, the dark, foreboding side of his complex personality was about to be awakened.

As Snag and Agitatin' Bill were passing by an old panel truck someone used as a place for sleep, they heard a child's muffled scream. Without a second thought Snag jerked open the door, revealing a slight-framed figure. He was engaged in an unpardonable act, against what appeared to be a seven-year-old boy.

The next scene was an illustrated portrait of the fate of a transgressor, painted blood red and black and blue. Snag held the terrified perpetrator with one huge hand while he brutally bashed him with the other hand.

"Go get Willie and the rest of the carneys. We're gonna make sure he never touches another child,"

With It—For It—and Up Against It

Snag declared, as he looked menacingly at what was left of the molester's face. "He's not gonna hurt anyone again. I'm gonna see to that," he snarled.

Agitatin' Bill was frightened; he'd never seen Snag so furious. "God, help me find Willie and some of the carneys," he mumbled, as he ran up the midway.

The following day Johnny opened his trailer door and discovered a fleet of police cars, an ambulance and a large crowd of people assembled down by the tilt-a-whirl trailer. As he drew near, he saw Noble Fairly with his hand resting on a police officer's shoulder, speaking into the officer's ear. Someone or something was wrapped in a body bag lying next to the rear wheels of the tilt trailer. Snag Hughes, who was the foreman on the tilt-a-whirl, was giving his statement to one of the officers.

Johnny walked up beside Willie, the electrician, and asked, "What's going on?"

Willie answered without ever looking at Johnny, "That fellow laid down between the wheels of the tilt trailer in a sleeping bag and went to sleep. Snag moved the tilt trailer this morning. He had no idea anyone was under there. Looks like that fellow will be sleeping for a long time."

Something about the whole scene troubled Johnny Palmer, especially the report that fell from Willie's lips. It was not the words. It was not the deadpan way he said the words. It was the atmosphere around the words — cold, calculating, judgmental, premeditated. One or all of these words were not enough to describe the vengeance and death that stirred in the air. It was thick and troubling and final.

Not much else was said. Arrangements were made for the body to be shipped to a specified address. The police had ignored the disfigured face of the dead man, preferring to close the matter — clean and quick. After all he was not one of their citizens. He was one of them. Let the carneys handle it. One less carnie here or there mattered little to the authorities.

As quickly as the rain came, just as quickly it was gone. The last days of the fair were jam packed with people, and profits were close to last year's figures. The show had closed for the night. Many of the carneys were standing outside the office trailer cuttin' up jackpots (spinning yarns and telling tales).

Everyone was relieved that the rain had ended. "The Lord makes it rain on the just and the unjust," Don Brown celebrated in a loud voice, "which illustrates God's desire to bless all men including carneys." He crow hopped about in an uncoordinated dance of praise. Most of the carneys just looked at him in a curious way. They didn't know if he was right or not. One thing they were sure of, Don Brown believed it.

The show made a 'circus move' to the next fair. (A 'circus move' meant the carnival closed, tore down that night, moved to the next fair, set up and opened that same day.)

With It—For It—and Up Against It

The midway was packed and business was good. Everyone had made the opening, everyone, except Dr. Dubious. His main attraction, John Wesley, who was supposed to be buried in the grave, was drunk. Not only was he drunk, he was walking around the midway carrying a Gideon Bible. He was preaching with a fanatical fervor that was most compelling. He had punctuated his sermon with such rigorous body language he was exhausted.

He had gathered quite a crowd. It was obvious, that sometime in his life, he had been exposed to the teaching of the word of God. "Repent and be saved, you generation of unbelievers," he roared, with inebriated enthusiasm.

Unable to steady himself, he had braced his back against one side of the Ferris wheel ticket box. He had delivered his sermon with great passion. There was so much spittle on his face he appeared to be foaming at the mouth. Indeed he had made a spectacle of himself for the cause of Christ.

Silvia Brown almost passed by the flawed figure and the sizeable flock he'd been entertaining. By now his voice was spent, his strength depleted, the despair of his heart surfaced in heaving sobs. When she heard his excessive wail, her heart went out to him. She had never seen such a tormented young man. He was undone, alone and without God.

Sylvia walked up to the exhausted orator, put her arm around him and asked, "What's your name son? Where did you come from?"

Without warning, the young man crumpled in her arms. Silvia struggled to keep him on his feet.

With It—For It—and Up Against It

Someone in the crowd came to her aid, "Let me have him ma'am. He's going to hurt you. He's too heavy for you."

Grateful for the relief, Silvia complied and looked into the face of Malcolm Wright. He looked terrible. It was not that he was disheveled or dirty. Quite the opposite, he was clean and well groomed but his features were drawn and impaired. He looked weaker than the man he was attempting to help did.

Together they were able to ascertain the place of his employment. Dr. Dubious met them in front of the show tent and said, "John, why do you do this to yourself?" John gave no reply. He then lifted the canvas and assisted them as they struggled to deliver their impaired cargo.

They left the young man in the care of his employer who was anxious to sober him up. Without him, he didn't have a show. He would have to remain closed.

After leaving Dr. Dubious to attend the young man, Silvia and Malcolm continued down the midway. Silvia had been shocked at his appearance. "Lord, please help me to be a blessing to Malcolm," she softly prayed. As they came to the office trailer, Malcolm asked, "Would you mind coming in for a minute? I'm aware of your family and the way you conduct yourself. Right now I need someone to talk to. I can't think of anyone I trust more than you."

Inside the trailer, Silvia seated herself and watched Malcolm as he sank into his office chair. He looked like he had aged twenty years in the last few days.

"Silvia, I need help. I have managed to stay away from the gin, but there's still something missing. I have been experiencing these strange dreams, not only that, I'm seeing things, hearing things. I haven't slept since I quit drinking and that's been more than a week. I feel like I'm losing control.

"As you know, my mother died three years before my dad did. She was in a sanitarium and didn't where she was or who she was. It could be I'm losing my mind. What do you think I need to do?" Malcolm asked, as innocently as a child would.

"Malcolm, I don't know what you need to do, but I know Someone who does. Every problem I've ever had, He has been able to solve. What you need, what everyone needs, is Jesus. "If I may, I'd like to share our family's testimony," Silvia said, as she looked directly into Malcolm's haggard face.

"About ten years ago, Don, Pumpkin, Dallas and I were living in Oklahoma. Don worked for a car dealership as a salesman. People liked him. They also trusted him. He worked hard and became very successful. He also picked up some bad habits. Drinking was at the top of the list. The environment in our home was a disaster. We never knew what kind of condition Don would come home in. It was a real problem. Drink was destroying our marriage and our home and our lives.

"Don drank to solve the turmoil within his soul. With all he had achieved, with all he had accomplished, success and financial security had been unable to fill the empty caverns of his heart. He tried to reform. He was still miserable. What he needed

With It—For It—and Up Against It

— what he longed for was fellowship with God, the peace of God and the purpose of God working in his life."

Silvia paused a moment, reflecting on those painful times and hoping Malcolm's heart was open to receive what she was about to share.

"Out of the clear blue sky, Don's boss came by our house one night and witnessed to Don and our entire family. He shared with us how man was created to have fellowship with God. That fellowship had been broken in the Garden of Eden, when God's crowning creation, Adam and Eve, sinned. God sent his only son, Jesus Christ, to save man from his sin and restore a right relationship with God. He told us that sin meant being separated from God and his wonderful plan for our lives.

"Don's boss went on to explain how Jesus died on the cross to pay the penalty for our sins. After his death, they placed him in a tomb. In three days he arose from the dead. Because Jesus was made alive we could be born again.

"He led us in a simple prayer acknowledging Jesus as our only Saviour and Lord. Don, Pumpkin, Dallas and myself accepted Jesus and invited him to take control of our lives. Our home, our family and our lives were dramatically changed that wonderful night." Silvia's spirit soared within her as she recalled this most precious time in her life. Oh, to be able to share Jesus with Malcolm, to see God work in his life as he had done in theirs.

Malcolm had listened to every word. He knew Silvia believed what she was saying. It was difficult for him to understand that all you had to do was pray a simple prayer. Surely there was more to it than that. He felt the need to somehow earn the right to be saved, to make restitution for his sin, to become good enough to be acceptable in the sight of God. But how? He'd done his very best and he was getting worse.

It was at this moment, he felt an inward stirring in his soul. He couldn't explain it, but he was certain something, or someone, was dealing with him. From the depths of his being, he suddenly wanted to rid himself of the habits and attitudes that were destroying him.

Perhaps this is what it's like when you have a mental breakdown, he reasoned within himself. Tears coursed down his face. Despair tore at his heart. He felt an agony of soul that was unbearable. Then, without further evaluation, he heard himself cry out, "Lord, help me! Lord, help me!"

In that moment of surrender, he experienced the inward working of God's Holy Sprit. Instantaneously, he knew he had been changed, he knew he was forgiven. He knew that Jesus Christ was Lord of his life.

What he had been unable to do in a lifetime of trying, Jesus had done in a moment of time. He would never be the same. It was stupendous! Marvelous!

Silvia wept tears of joy as she witnessed Malcolm's glorious transformation. The glory of God illuminated his face, he radiated with the touch of heaven. It was quite dramatic — new and marvelous. Jesus came to seek and to save the lost. Today, one who was lost had been found and of all people, a carney - a drunkard. Saved, by His power divine. Saved, to new life sublime. Saved! Saved! Saved!

Silvia knew that Malcolm, like all young Christians, needed instruction and discipling. He needed to understand what he had done. Christianity wasn't like other religions. Salvation comes by grace through Christ and Him crucified. In other religions, salvation comes by works and man is glorified. You can believe that the Bible is the word of God without trusting God for your salvation. You can believe in the deity of Christ without receiving him as your personal Savior. You can believe in salvation by Christ's grace without appropriating his saving grace for your own salvation.

The foundation for the saving of your soul is faith in God — faith in Jesus and his death on the cross — faith in his resurrection from the dead — faith in the resurrection power of God is essential for salvation. "Nothing in my hand I bring, simply to thy cross I cling." Faith is the opposite of works. You are saved because of who you know, not what you know.

You can be a biblical scholar and fail to understand that all men are saved by God's amazing grace. You could be an individual who was so illiterate you couldn't read your own name in boxcar letters. But to your credit, you were brilliant enough to invite Jesus into your life and accept him as your own personal Savior.

All these truths and more Silvia shared. She knew they were necessary to insure that Malcolm grew in faith and in the knowledge of the Lord.

She was elated with Malcolm's decision. She said goodbye and hurried to the custard stand. She could hardly wait to share the good news with her family.

Johnny had made the circus move without incident. He was reminded to do a little mechanical work on his Buick. He wasn't going to drive that roadmaster another mile until he aimed those headlights. He had opened the hood and was busily examining the best way to accomplish this necessary task.

His thoughts were on Pumpkin. He had tried to improve their tumultuous relationship. Each time he had asked her to go somewhere with him, she was always busy.

Lately, she was hardly speaking to him. "I thought Christians were supposed to be forgiving," he muttered, as he removed one of the headlight rings.

"Hey, buddy old pal," Happy Parks said, with an energetic emphasis, as he walked up behind Johnny. "Got troubles have you?" Happy asked, as he looked at the raised hood on the Buick.

"No, I'm doing something I should have done six months ago. I'm aiming these aggravating headlights," Johnny answered, as he gave Happy a friendly smile.

"Shouldn't you be doing this in the dark? How are you going to know where your lights are shining if you can't see them?" Happy asked, as he roughly shoved on Johnny's shoulder.

"Anything I do to these headlights will be an improvement. I'll tell you something else. I have

With It—For It—and Up Against It

X-ray eyes just like Superman. Not only that, I'm sure you couldn't do any better in the dark!" Johnny declared, in a superior manner while he waved his screwdriver at Happy.

Johnny, as well as everyone else, knew Happy could fix or repair anything, which made his statement all the more humorous and offensive — just as he had intended.

The upkeep and maintenance on Happy's penny arcade machines would drive most folks insane. To Happy, it was child's play.

"How about we go over to the beer tent and get us a cold brew and a beer cheese sandwich," Happy suggested, as he rubbed his rock hard stomach. "They just happen to have an outstanding polka band. That and the service make the sandwiches taste all the better. There's a sweet little German gal who's taken a liking to me. Can you imagine that?" Happy asked, as he raised his eyebrow in a quizzical arch.

"She must be blind and desperate is all I can say. Probably old enough to be your mother. Not only that, I'm not as fond of those stinky sandwiches as you are. I wouldn't mind a cold brew. I should be finished right here in a minute," Johnny declared, as he turned the last screw into the headlight ring.

The beer tent was crowded and the band was playing loud. Johnny and Happy found a table off to one side. Immediately a healthy looking waitress swept up to their table. "Come back again did you? Is it the sandwiches or my charming disposition you're so fond of?" She looked directly at Happy.

"I couldn't stay away. Every time I'd think about your feminine charms, I got hungry. The contrasting aromas of the beer cheese and your beautiful fragrance has cast a spell on me. Who knew hunger pangs could make someone like me so happy." With that, he pulled a chair up to the tab le for her.

"I'll set down, but only for a minute. It's three more hours before my shift ends. Can't make the boss mad, even if he is my brother," she laughingly declared, as she tossed her blond hair in a comical gesture.

Now, this is the girl of my dreams, Happy thought, as he looked at her abundant benefits. She was tall and embraceable. A picture of good health, she was not fat or thin. To him she was just perfect. He wouldn't mind settling down with a woman like her. He liked 'em big and healthy and she filled the bill.

"Greta, this is my good friend Johnny Palmer. Johnny, this is the best thing I've found in the dairy state." Happy boastfully announced, as he gave Greta a big hug. "Say hello to Greta Lomiller." They exchanged pleasantries, then Greta made her way to the bar and placed their order.

"Well, Happy, it looks like you're after more than a brew and a beer cheese sandwich. What's filling up the inside of your lovesick head? Is this the one?" Johnny enjoyed watching Happy squirm in his seat.

"I'm not for sure but I tell you one thing, if she's not the one, she could easily make me forget to look for the one who is." Happy impulsively whacked the tabletop for emphasis with his tattooed hand.

With It—For It—and Up Against It

"Don't go punishing yourself lover boy. It appears to me, you need to get better acquainted with this dairyland beauty," Johnny said encouragingly.

"That's the most sensible thing you've said all day," Happy said as he looked for Greta to return. "Trouble is, her parents are unwilling to allow her to go out with me. She's younger than Pumpkin. They might consider letting her go on a double date," Happy stated, as he rolled his eyes in frustration.

Johnny wanted to help his friend. He wasn't sure what arrangements could be made. Who knows if I can help or not, Johnny thought. Pumpkin had refused to have anything to do with him lately. Maybe this is an opportunity to get her down off her high horse. I'll make an attempt. In fact, I think I'll do it right now. If she doesn't respond, I don't know what I'll tell Happy, he reflected as he looked at his friend.

He hurried through his meal, sure that Happy and Greta wouldn't mind a few minutes at the table by themselves. "Don't let him get his nose too far down in that beer mug," Johnny teased, as he said goodbye.

He left the beer tent to find Pumpkin and try to settle their differences. His first stop was the custard stand. Don informed him she was probably at their house trailer. Winding back behind the joints, Johnny spotted the Brown's house trailer and Pumpkin at the same time. She was just going in the door carrying a basket full of clothes. She had been to the local laundry mat; a task she was assigned to do each week.

"Need some help?" he inquired, as he smiled at her.

With It—For It—and Up Against It

"Now you show up! There's never a man around when you need him," she declared, as she placed the last basket of clothes in the trailer.

"I would have been here sooner if I had known you were hiring help," Johnny teased, as he reached for her hand. Her skin was cool and smooth. "Come outside for a minute. I'd like to talk to you, if I may. We never seem to be able to get together. All of a sudden you're too busy."

She was startled that he was so abrupt. No pleasantries, no idle conversation, he was focused and straight to the point. Perhaps she had been too withdrawn. Had she overplayed her hand? Had she gone too far? She was about to find out. She felt a little frightened and disturbed.

"Pumpkin, I've come to settle our differences if I can. I want you to understand I am not an infatuated schoolboy. I have deep feelings for you. I have attempted to make up for my preoccupation with business and other interests. Up until now, you have not responded in a positive or polite way," Johnny continued. I don't want to be cruel or unkind. However, I want you to understand, I don't intend to pursue this relationship any further unless we can come to some kind of agreement."

Johnny hated having this conversation. He wanted her more than anyone he'd ever met. He knew he loved her. He also knew he couldn't live with himself if he became a weak-minded lovesick fool. He would rather end their relationship than chase after her like a love-starved slave. To act in such a manner was unmanly. He would not entertain or tolerate that kind of behavior out of others, let alone himself.

Pumpkin listened as he informed her of his feelings. He spoke softly and kindness settled on each syllable. She felt ashamed that she had been so hateful and self-centered. She had been less than what was expected of a Christian. She was grateful for the opportunity to make things right. She had prayed for a husband. She believed he was the answer to her prayer. Knowing this, why had she acted like a spoiled schoolgirl? At times, she didn't know her own mind.

"Johnny, I don't know what you mean when you say you have deep feelings for me? I've been totally confused. You've made little time for me from the beginning," she said softly. Even then you were moody and distant. I thought the thing to do was give you time. Not being with you has been torture for me. Believe me, I've been very unhappy," she advised as tears filled her eyes.

"It's true; I have been ignoring you. I'm asking you to forgive me. I want to be with you." Before she could say anything more, Johnny grabbed her up in his arms and tenderly and passionately kissed her. It was wonderful, so much so, he did it again and again and again. She was like a narcotic. He couldn't get enough of her. She was gasping as she held tightly to him. She had never known such intense emotions. She felt both elation and alarm. Somehow, this must stop. But how?

They were lost together in an all-encompassing passion. They were locked in a blissful moment of incalculable intensity.

With It—For It—and Up Against It

Johnny tore himself away from her embrace. A moment longer a door would have opened he wouldn't have had the will to close. He had never known such urgency — such desire.

Pumpkin smoothed the front of her dress and looked at him in wide-eyed amazement. She had never experienced such breathtaking enchantment. She had lost herself in his arms. She was bewildered. "If this were a Clark Gable movie, we'd be smoking a cigarette about now," she nervously stated, as she tried to bring levity to their situation.

Johnny roared with laughter, breaking the tension of the moment. Pumpkin's observations of the movies were so out of character for her. He couldn't suppress the merriment it had engendered.

She was gorgeous, sensual, witty and intelligent. He decided, right then and there, he was going to marry her. It sounded strange to him, but he knew it was true. She was everything he wanted and more.

"How about you and I go over to the beer tent? There's someone I'd like to introduce you to." He gave her an affectionate hug.

CHAPTER SIX

~~~

Pollock loved the rough, rapid life of the carnival. He wasn't an educated man. He liked things simple and had little need for creature comforts. In some circles, he would have been known as a minimalist. He had few friends and fewer hangouts, one of those being the AT Show.

The At Show was short for Athletic Show. Red O'Grady ran a stable of grunt and groan boys (wrestlers and boxers who took on all challengers.)

It can be argued that professional wrestling was birthed in the carnival AT Show. One thing was sure, it was a tough way to make a living.

The wrestlers often had backgrounds in college wrestling. The boxers usually came out of golden gloves. Some athletes did both boxing and wrestling, but all the fighters came to him as amateurs until Red trained them and said otherwise.

Red was tougher than rawhide leather; a tall, rawboned redheaded professional wrestler who was

With It—For It—and Up Against It

fearless. Even though he was past his prime, training with him was no picnic. More than one of his students had found himself either pinned or howling in pain from a submission hold. He delighted in inflicting pain upon what he called "fresh meat." If you couldn't take it, you couldn't stay.

The key to big grosses on an At Show was the ability to build heat, meaning the fighter was gifted in aggravation. He had to have the courage and audacity to make the paying public furious with him and everyone connected with the AT Show.

A local fighter or wrestler usually well known, sometimes a celebrity, would agree to wrestle or fight the carney. Standing outside on the bally platform the contestants would agree to the rules of the contest and the amount of the winner's purse. It was here that Red's training was most notable; the loudmouthed carney wrestler would scream and shout, taunt and question the ancestry of his opponent. Anything he said or did to upset the audience was a plus. His conceit and flamboyant confidence always infuriated the potential ticket purchaser.

After nearly coming to blows onstage, the combatants would agree to immediately settle the matter inside the ring. By now the public was outraged. They couldn't wait to purchase a ticket and support their local hero. They also wanted to make sure the sorry old loudmouthed carney got his comeuppance.

One of the most profitable parts of this make-believe dispute was the additional cash generated. The fight always ended in controversy. These same ticket purchasers would be swept outside to buy another ticket to witness the fight to end all fights. In and out the crowd would be worked, fight after fight until they had spent the bigger part of the night, and no small amount of cash, to witness a fight whose outcome was predetermined days in advance. To their delight, the local hero would always prevail. The two fighters, by now, were the best of friends — a bond of friendship made more secure by the abundance of cash that was divided between them.

Red saw Pollock when he came into the tent and he wasn't particularly pleased to see him. Red didn't like bullies and he had hopes of one day having a "training session" with the big Pollock. He would love to teach him the difference between a tough street fighter and a trained professional. He could show him more tricks than a monkey could with a hundred foot rope.

It was a couple of hours before opening the show. Some of the wrestlers were training, stretching and doing various exercises.

During the fair season, Red tried to carry at least three fighters, presently, he had four. He had picked up a good-looking prospect last week who had already shown promise as a tough wrestler. He was surprisingly adept at stirring up the crowd — natural born showman. The combination of skill and box office appeal was a rare find. Red felt he might have a future champion on his hands.

Pollock looked at Red and said, "I was in last night and watched your new boy. Clean the baby fat off of him and he might make it," Pollock stated, with an air of expertise. Red grunted and wondered where Pollock got the idea he was a talent scout. *He wouldn't know a wristlock from a wristwatch*, Red thought as he picked up a stack of towels.

"He's young, still in his teens, but he's got heart. You don't wanna' mess with him," Red declared with a voice of certainty. Pollock was amused with Red's confident tone. What did he know about his skills as a fighter? It might not even be a contest. He hadn't been in the ring, but he'd been around. So far, he was undefeated and he didn't see that changing anytime soon.

Red was in one of his grumpier moods. Pollock decided he had better things to do than hang around an old has-been like him. He would like to see Dixie. *She seems to be avoiding me*, he pondered, as he walked out of the AT Show and headed toward the office trailer, thinking Dixie might have gone there to see Malcolm. As he approached the front of the office trailer, he saw Noble going into the side door of Malcolm's office. She's not here Pollock ventured and chose the cookhouse as the next place to look.

Malcolm was glad to see Noble and said as much in a welcoming tone. They were close to the same age, but somehow he always regarded Noble as a father figure, rather than just a friend.

He hadn't told Dixie about his salvation experience, although he wanted to. He couldn't find the right words. He had rehearsed it in his mind, but couldn't get the words out of his mouth. He wasn't sure she would understand. He wasn't all that certain he understood. What he was sure of was, something wonderful had happened to him.

With It — For It — and Up Against It

Noble poured himself a cup of coffee and sat down on the couch. "Thought I'd come by and give you the good news. The fair committee has renewed our contract for five more years. All in all, they were quite complimentary. I also learned that two other carnivals had approached them about making a change. This is really getting to be a cutthroat business," Noble said in an informative way.

"Another thing in our favor was the wonderful relationship your father had with one of the older members of the fair board," Noble stated, as he reached in the humidor for a Cuban cigar.

Malcolm sat there trying to focus on what Nobel was saying. At another time this would have been the greatest news in the world. Right now all Malcolm could think about was how he was going to make Noble understand what had happened to him.

"Noble, I know I've been acting like a fool these past few years. I want you to know my drinking and the irresponsible management of this show are over. Without your constant vigilance, I don't know what might have become of the carnival and everyone involved. I owe you a great debt of gratitude," Malcolm declared with sincerity. "I've received a new lease on life. How do I tell you; I've been changed and for the first time in a long time I'm in my right mind," Malcolm spoke in a soft voice, as he searched Noble's face for a sign that he understood.

Noble understood all right, in fact, he was way ahead of Malcolm. "What you're telling me is, you've had some kind of religious enlightenment," Noble stated, as he rose up from the couch.

Malcolm was shocked at Noble's keen perception. How could he possibly come to the heart of this matter so quickly? "How did you know?" Malcolm asked incredulously.

"Hell, man! I was raised in the Lutheran Church. My dear old daddy was on the board of trustees. Mother carried me to Sunday school in diapers. The only book I've studied more than Law has been the Bible. I'll tell you this, if you're planning on living the life of a Christian, let me set your mind at ease, I'm all for it," Noble announced with confidence. "I've never met a man, anywhere at anytime, who was sorry he had given his life to Jesus Christ," he continued. "I've met more than a few, including myself, who regretted leaving the narrow path of redemption to travel the broad road of destruction," Noble assured Malcolm, as he poured himself another cup of coffee.

"Have you told Dixie?" Malcolm flinched when Noble made his inquiry. A student of human nature, Noble knew the answer by Malcolm's body language.

Noble, in a fatherly manner asked, "What are you going to do? You have to tell her. She's got to know. Who knows, this might be just the thing to patch up your difficulties. You don't want to wait too long," Noble counseled, as he observed a nervous twitch in Malcolm's face.

Malcolm knew Noble was right. He had to tell Dixie, but how? The possibility of her rejection made him nauseous. This time it wasn't because he was drying out. It was a different kind of queasiness. This had nothing to do with his body craving alcohol.

Malcolm knew he had ignored her for years, now all of sudden; he was terrified at the prospect of losing her. Could he find a way to make things right? His mind raced with thoughts, ideas, anything that would convey his affirmation of love, anything to open her eyes to the truth of his love for her and to his new-found faith.

"Malcolm, perhaps I can talk to her, kinda prepare the way. I've always hoped you two would mend your differences," Noble volunteered. "I can remember the early days, right before the trial, you two couldn't get enough of each other. It was a beautiful thing to see," Noble said as he thoughtfully looked at Malcolm and waited for a response.

"I appreciate your offer, but this is something I have to do myself. It's my fault our marriage failed. It's up to me to make things right," he allowed as his face took on a serious aspect.

Hearing that, Nobel abruptly walked to the door, saying in parting, "Well, I got other fish to fry. If I can help in any way, just give me a call."

Malcolm stared after him as he walked out the door. Other than Dixie, Noble was his most valued friend. Maybe now would be a good time to talk to Dixie, he mused as he walked out of the office.

Happy Parks, well . . . Happy wasn't happy. Tomorrow was slough night, (the night the carnival was dismantled and moved to the next fair.) His time with Greta had been limited. Theirs had been a torrid relationship. Greta had made time for him without her

With It—For It—and Up Against It

parents' consent. Sadly, she had to involve her brother in their charade. Their stolen moments together had only intensified their passion. They were in love; that was certain.

The double date with Johnny and Pumpkin had not materialized. Greta's parents wouldn't even consider allowing her to go out with Happy.

It was obvious that they believed all carneys were tramps, bums and convicted felons. Would they be surprised when they learned that Happy was a college graduate and had been raised in a family of intellectuals.

Greta had stated her determination to leave with him tomorrow night. If she had to choose between her parents' love and Happy's love, she had adamantly declared, it was no contest. She wanted to be with him, whatever the cost, marriage or no marriage. Happy was opposed to such an inappropriate arrangement. He was ready and willing to marry her. He was unwilling to turn her into what was called, in the carnival world, a possum belly broad. (Possum belly was a slang term for storage bins built about twelve to twenty inches off the ground, in front of the back wheels of a trailer or truck.) It was usually large enough to sleep inside. Females, who ran off with the carnival, often found themselves forsaking their virtue inside these compartments.

What Greta's parents, as well as the world didn't know, was the fact that many of the carneys had more honor and character than their hometown Lodge Hall brother had. They most assuredly practiced a loyalty and closed-mouthed allegiance within the carnival that was missing in most hometowns.

On the other hand, they were a rough and tumble lot who lived free and independent. Most resented being tied down to living in one location. The love of the road was a constant addiction that fed their quest for adventure and financial reward.

Happy decided it was time to try and find a solution to their situation. Greta would be ending her shift in about ten minutes. He was grateful she'd be free. They desperately needed to talk. The difference in these hometown employees and carneys was, the carneys worked from "can 'til can't," or from the opening to the closing of the carnival.

Happy had retained his love of beer, but his appetite for beer cheese sandwiches had abated. It might be another year before one of those sandwiches would look good to him, he thought, as he headed toward the beer tent.

Greta was waiting impatiently for six o' clock to arrive, so she was more than delighted to see Happy walk into the tent. Ignoring the summons of one of her customers, she rushed up to Happy, and to his embarrassment, kissed him in a most passionate way.

"Hey picture boy, how'd you like the special beer tent welcome?" she asked, as she escorted him to his favorite table. Without waiting, in a much more serious tone, she asked the question that had been on her mind these last few days, "Are you going to take me with you?"

Happy was dumbfounded. He didn't want to leave her, but he wouldn't subject her to an illicit affair. It wasn't right. It wasn't in him to ruin her good name. He loved her too much to soil her reputation. They both wanted children. This had to be done correctly, with a license and a legal ceremony. There was only one answer, might as well sound it out! "What would you say if I asked you to marry me?" he mumbled as he watched her eyes fill with tears.

It was more than she had hoped for. She would have given anything just to be with him. Greta was elated! "Yes, yes, oh yes! I'll marry you! Today, tonight, whenever, and where ever! I'm yours for all eternity," she vowed, with a voice filled with reverence and commitment.

Happy forgot about the crowd milling about them and wrapped his arms around her in a most enthusiastic embrace. "Too bad we don't have time to celebrate," whirling Greta in a tight circle.

There was a lot to be done in a short amount of time. They discussed their plans at great length. There was the matter of informing Greta's parents. He wasn't going to steal away with her, like a thief in the night. They wanted a proper ceremony. Like all brides, Greta desired to have her family present.

They decided the wedding would be in six days. Happy would come back next week for the wedding. Their honeymoon would be spent on the carnival lot, working in the penny arcade. It wasn't terribly romantic, but extremely practical under the circumstances.

Happy and Greta agreed that when the season was over, they would travel to some exotic place and officially celebrate their matrimonial bliss. What was uppermost in their minds was working toward a common goal to insure they would be together. If they never had a planned honeymoon, it would make little difference to them.

Greta drew her brother aside and told him the wonderful news. He was a large jovial man who appreciated the predicament his sister was in. He was only too glad to aid them in their marital plans. He liked Happy and had volunteered to speak to his parents on their behalf. Happy offered his thanks but was convinced it was only proper for him to inform the Lomillers of their engagement and subsequent marriage.

He thought it wise to honor their traditions, so he intended to ask for Greta's hand as a gesture of respect. Equally true, he had no intention of allowing anyone to hinder or cancel their plans. With or without her parent's blessing, they were going to be married.

Johnny saw Happy walking toward the beer tent. He decided to allow Happy to continue his courting without company. Instead Johnny elected to stop by the cookhouse for a cup of coffee. Bill Charity, looking tired and angry sat down at his table. "Half the help in the kitchen quit last night," he said. "You carry them all spring so when the fair season starts you'll have plenty of help. What do they do? They get smashed! I'm still holding a lot of their paychecks. I'm hoping when they sober up they'll come back," he remarked, as he stared wearily at the kitchen trailer.

"Its back to me and momma, just like the old days." Bill looked at Johnny for some kind of response, but he remained quiet without making any comment.

Through the front of the cookhouse walked a familiar looking woman. Her hair, although it was bleached blond, was dirty and disheveled. Her face and figure was old way before its time. The features of her face, once beautiful, were disfigured. She had a number of scars over one eye and her nose appeared to have been broken several times. Her complexion was pale and sickly. Obviously, she was in poor health, but her appearance stated that poor health was just part of her problem; she looked like she had been to hell and back.

She walked tall and straight, the refined coordinated stride of a dancer shouted out her life's work. Her body was thin and deficient, yet there remained the memory of a voluptuous figure. Johnny was fascinated as he watched her sit down at a table, knowing he was supposed to know her. But she didn't look like the girl he remembered.

"Bill, who is that woman that just walked in?"

"That's a sad story. You know her Johnny. That's Sadie Kerr! You remember, she was the biggest star in burlesque. She worked the big State Fairs for the largest show in the world, United of America shows. She was known as Carmel Colt, the girl with the 45's. Don't you remember her popularity rose to such heights she left the road and was a featured attraction in New Orleans, Las Vegas, Chicago, New York and who knows where else. She was big! Somewhere on the road to fame she was introduced to smack (heroin.) Near the end, they say she was shootin' up thousands of dollars of dope every week. She partnered up with a sadistic, small time dope dealer who got his jollies out of inflicting pain and suffering. Her career went down faster than a fifty-pound hailstone. One day she was on top of the world. The next day she was a "has been" with a high dollar habit. She tracked up her arms. He trashed her face. They terminated her life, all but the little you now see," Bill seemed even more depressed as he finished his recollections of Sadie.

Johnny was brimming with questions but he wasn't sure Bill was up to answering them. It was almost as if Bill read his mind. "Someone told me she came over here from the United Shows," Bill continued. "There's an agent on one of Don Patton's joints that is said to be living with her. She comes in for coffee, once in awhile, but she seldom eats anything. My wife is worried about her," Bill said seriously. "She appears to need medical help. That needle is a scourge of suffering and a scaffold of savagery. It will end her life if she doesn't get some help."

Bill sat silent for a few moments as his eyes stared vacantly into his own troubled past. He had more than a spectator's view of the tragedies of a junkie's life. The despair and destruction of his youth was concealed under the long sleeved shirts he always wore. Hidden beneath the white cloth were the telltale signs of the needle's furious imprint that revealed its malicious madness.

His abhorrent subjugation to heroin's grip upon his sanity and soul was not easily forsaken. He had been clean and free of its viperous sting for more than

With It—For It—and Up Against It

twenty years. His wife put it best; he was too tough to die. Instead, she said his sentence was to operate a carnival cookhouse. That should more than make up for my misspent youth, he thought as a smile creased his tanned face.

Johnny quietly slipped out of the cookhouse as Bill continued his private thoughts into yesteryear's partnership with pain. He almost missed seeing Pumpkin as he hurried toward the cork gallery. The loud wailing of a young child directed his attention toward the middle of the midway. There stood Pumpkin with a frightened toddler who was shrieking and shaking with terror.

"Hey mister, can you help me find this sweet baby's parents?" inquired Pumpkin, a smile of relief lighting up her face as she held tightly to the small child's hand.

The little castaway was stained and streaked with grape snow cone juice, pink cotton candy sugars and yellow hot dog mustard. His eyes were blood red from sobbing and crying. "I want my mommy," he screamed! He was a pitiful little figure. His face and clothes were colored with every carnival treat imaginable. Sadly, those stains would not help identify him.

Pumpkin had no idea how long he had been separated from his mother. She had involved herself in his terrified flight as he ran down the midway searching for his mother.

Johnny was only too glad to assist Pumpkin. "The best thing to do is take him to the Grandstand ticket office. They have a facility set aside to help in locating

With It—For It—and Up Against It

and claiming the lost. See if you can get him to tell you his name," Johnny suggested, as they endeavored to calm down the frightened little boy. Pumpkin kept up a steady conversation with the child, assuring him everything was going to be all right.

They walked toward the Grandstand as rapidly as the boy's stride would allow. By the time they got there, they were able to give the authorities the name of the child. His name and description were then broadcast over an intricate network of loud speakers that covered the entire expanse of the fairgrounds.

After what seemed a lifetime to the child, the frantic and teary-eyed mother rushed into the office and gratefully claimed the lost child.

Johnny listened in awe as that mother offered up words of thanksgiving and praise to heaven in a prayer humbly and reverently sounded aloud for all to hear. To witness the joy and beauty of that reunion was priceless. The blissful countenance of mother and child is a memory to be inscribed upon the hallway of any man's heart. The relieved mother clung to her child as she expressed her overwhelming gratitude to Pumpkin and Johnny.

Johnny felt the need to leave before he got as misty-eyed as the women had. He hurriedly walked out of the office as he choked back a tear. Pumpkin was wiping tears from her eyes as she witnessed his rapid departure. She thought it would be best to wait a moment before she followed after him.

When Pumpkin came out to meet him, he had regained his composure. "How about going with me down to the cork gallery? That's where I was headed when I saw you," he said quietly, as he watched her touch up her makeup.

"I need to check on Popsicle and the rest of the agents. Bennie is supposed to be taking care of business, but you never know what may be going on," he said wearily. "I just need to make an appearance."

"I need to get back to the custard stand and give Dallas a break, but I suppose it won't hurt him to wait a little while," Pumpkin ventured as she took hold of Johnny's arm.

He was just about to ask her a question when all of a sudden the crowded midway parted as if directed by an invisible hand. Running up the midway was a rotund man about six feet tall. His broad face was covered in blood. His eyes, black from some well placed punches, were swelling shut with each rapid stride. The front portion of his shirt was torn and most of the buttons were missing, exposing a bulging belly and a sagging chest. His face was framed with fear. The heaving, heavy sobbing search for oxygen emanating from his nostrils signaled his lungs desperate desire for rest and relief.

Just then the purveyor of his terror appeared; a huge man, infuriated and about to catch his fleeing prey to administer his self adjudged punishment a second time. Pollock seized the shirt collar of his badly beaten foe. With one powerful jerk of his muscular arm, he slammed the exhausted man's body violently to the ground. "Try and steal my ride help," he snarled as he brutally dragged the helpless perpetrator down the midway. "You'll think a long time before you show your face around here again,"

Pollock bellered as he stopped and hammered the man's face with his rock hard fists. "What made you think you could come on this show lot and hire all my ride help? You're too stupid to live," he screamed at the fallen figure. The battered man, now unconscious, gave no reply.

CHAPTER 7

Noble Fairly was standing near the ambulance door as they placed the unconscious man inside. His head, now badly swollen, looked as big as a basketball.

Pollock was nowhere to be seen. Angry at his severe attack, Noble had banished him to the office trailer. Pollock had been surprised at Noble's pugnacious attitude. Still seething from his recent pummeling of the United Show's ride superintendent, he reluctantly complied.

"Time enough later to teach Noble some respect. He'll learn to handle me with kid gloves or pay the price," Pollock sullenly vowed, as he stomped up the steps of the office trailer.

The low guttural sound of the ambulance siren warned the gathering crowd to move aside as the driver accelerated the emergency vehicle out the gate and onto the highway.

With It—For It—and Up Against It

One of the policemen on duty walked over to Noble and asked, "How do you want to handle this? This fellow named Pollock, is he one of your people?" Noble would have loved to say no but knew it was his duty to arrange for all charges to be dismissed, quickly and painlessly and as soon as possible.

Noble watched as the ambulance disappeared out of sight and said, "The guy in the ambulance is an employee of United Shows. Apparently all of their ride help quit. He made the mistake of coming here and trying to hire our help. The big Pollock is one of our employees," Noble stated advisedly. "To say that he was offended with the actions of the other man is an understatement. The end result you saw being loaded into the ambulance," he continued.

"If possible, I believe it would be beneficial for both of us to conclude our conversation at the public relations trailer. How long have you been on the force?" Noble asked the officer, as he guided him down the midway.

After some flattering remarks and a few key questions, Noble ascertained the policeman's willingness to cooperate. These kinds of incidents were best left out of the newspaper. The officer was about to discover just how grateful Noble, as representative of Mighty Wright Show, could be. Once again he had fulfilled his job description.

Always one to mind his own business, Johnny left the scene of the fight. He preferred to avoid the speculation and outright gossip that accompany these kinds of occurrences. He said little as he walked Pumpkin to the custard stand and returned to the cork gallery.

The awning was up, but there was no sign of Popsicle. Potential customers were standing at the counter. One teenager was looking down the barrel of one of the air rifles. "How about you, sonny boy? Want to try and win a prize?" Johnny asked, as he searched for a nail apron to put change in.

"I've been ready. Load her up. I'm about to win a big one," the teenager boasted, as he aimed the air rifle at the hardest target. A thudding sound signaled Johnny that the boy was correct. He had won a big prize.

"Hey, look what he got! He won a big one! Who else wants to try their luck? Come in and win while the boss is gone!" Johnny called out, as the lucky player proudly showed his friends the huge teddy bear.

The crowd on the midway grew larger and larger. Johnny spent the next few hours loading air rifles and receiving the player's money. It was a most profitable time. He scarcely had time to wonder where Popsicle had gone.

Near closing time, Easy Money came by the cork gallery and informed Johnny he had seen Popsicle in the G top. "He was throwing money around like Royalty. He was also drunker than Cooter Bill! I tried to get him to leave but he said he hated to break up the game. I forget who told me but they said he'd had an unbelievable run of good luck. Money was hanging out of every pocket. That's dangerous among this herd of hard cases," Easy Money said miserably, as he walked away.

Johnny turned out the lights to the cork gallery and let the awning down. Bennie came by and finished closing up. He walked up the midway uncertain whether to look for Popsicle or not. *It might be easier to let Popsicle find him,* he thought as he picked up the night's take from the other two joints. He decided he'd much rather spend his time with Pumpkin than exercising a futile search for Popsicle.

As he approached the custard stand Shorty Yeager rushed up beside him and blurted out loudly, "They found Popsicle beat all to hell behind the G top. Happy and Bennie were trying to see how bad his injuries were. They sent me to find you. It's getting to where a man ain't safe anywhere," Shorty observed, in an agitated tone.

Johnny ran down the back of the midway, behind the office trailer, past the lush wagon and almost collided with Snag Hughes who was coming from the opposite direction. Happy was carrying Popsicle in his arms as he appeared from behind the G top.

"Johnny, it doesn't look good. We've been unable to find out anything. I don't know if he is conscious or not. He's looked at me with his eyes open but hasn't said a word. He hasn't responded to anything I've done," Happy advised, as he searched Johnny's face for instructions.

"Let's load him in my car and take him to the emergency room," Johnny directed, as he endeavored to relieve Happy of part of his burden. Together they placed Popsicle in the back seat of the Buick.

With It—For It—and Up Against It

Johnny started the engine, placed the transmission in drive and roared down the backside of the midway. Happy, seated to his right, was keeping a close watch on their incapacitated friend. Popsicle lay in the backseat staring blankly at the back window.

The roadmaster engine howled through the streets of the city, announcing to all the critical needs of its cargo. They arrived at the hospital in record time. The hospital emergency entrance hall looked like a war zone. People and patients were scattered about in no particular order. A small-dedicated staff was endeavoring to take care of the worst cases first. Johnny stopped a fast moving man dressed in hospital garb and informed him of Popsicle's need for medical attention.

"Bring him in and put him on that first table," the orderly instructed, as he hurried down the hall. Happy had managed to get him out of the car and had carried him through the emergency room doors.

"Johnny, this place is bloodier than a packing house killing floor," Happy grunted, as he placed Popsicle on the narrow bed.

After what seemed like an hour or more, a tired-eyed intern, who looked as though he should be at home doing high school assignments, gave Popsicle a quick glance. Taking a small penlight he looked carefully into the stricken man's eyes.

"What do you think, Doc? We've been trying to get him to give some kind of response. All he does is stare," Happy advised the young intern, as he continued his examination.

With It—For It—and Up Against It

"Has he been drinking and if so how much?" the intern asked, as he probed Popsicle's stomach and chest. "He's definitely had trauma to his head," he said, as he continued his examination.

Johnny, with a thoughtful look, replied, "We don't know exactly how much he's had to drink. You can be sure, it was a lot."

The doctor removed his stethoscope from around his neck and said, "It looks like he's going to need some tests and some extended care. One of you will need to go to the main lobby to the administrative desk, and arrange for him to be admitted," he instructed, as he signaled an orderly and informed him where to take the patient. In less than a minute Popsicle was rapidly rolling down the hallway and out of sight.

Hospital waiting rooms are never pleasant places to pass away the time. Those sentenced to sit and wait are always embroiled in crisis, calamity and chaos — expectant figures with worried faces leaping to their feet with each passing white robed hospital nurse, hoping to hear an encouraging word and often facing the possibility of counseled words of despair. They wait and they worry.

Johnny and Happy found seats on a well-worn couch in back of the room. The stale air in the room smelled of unwashed bodies, cigarette smoke and urgency.

On the midway it was past midnight and Shorty Yeager was standing in Malcolm's office. In machine-like monotones he informed Malcolm of the attack and transportation of Popsicle to the local hospital.

Malcolm couldn't believe that one day could have so many unexpected problems and challenges. First, there was the assault on the United Show's ride superintendent and now this.

Wearily he sank down in his office chair and said, "Shorty, if they haven't returned in the morning by ten o' clock, I want you go down to the hospital, locate Johnny, and find out all you can.

For now, it's time for all God's children to be in bed," Malcolm added softly. Shorty was startled at Malcolm's parting words. *Who knew what time God wanted people to be in bed? I sure don't,* he thought as he blinked in astonishment.

Back at the hospital, the hours dragged by. The people in the waiting room dwindled down to a handful. Happy managed to find a reasonably comfortable spot and was sleeping soundly. Johnny had insisted he should go back to the lot, but he had stubbornly refused.

Remaining awake, he assumed tests were continuing to be done. Little other information had been given. Nothing in the way of diagnoses or results of tests had been revealed.

Restless and tired of sitting, Johnny decided to check on the reckless fella from United Shows. After all, he was a member of the brotherhood of carneys. He walked down the hall to the nurse's station. A large matronly looking woman, sitting at a low counter, looked up from a pile of papers and asked, "Can I help you?"

"Yes ma'am," Johnny replied, as the nurse continued her paper work. "Could you tell me what

With It—For It—and Up Against It

room the man from the carnival is in?" he asked, as he informed her of the time of his arrival. "He was brought in early this afternoon around five o' clock."

"Are you a relative or friend of the family?" the nurse asked. "This is a Catholic hospital and the rules are very strict," she advised kindly, as she looked closely at Johnny as he gave an answer.

"No ma'am, I'm not. However, I know some of the people he knows. He's here alone, I'm sure they would want me to see about him." The nurse gave him a long searching look and decided she liked what she saw. "Young man, he's in room 456. When you go in, if he's asleep, please don't awaken him," she instructed as she pointed toward the correct door.

"No ma'am, I will be real quiet," he said, as he turned and walked down the corridor.

He opened the door marked 456 and quietly entered. The man lying on the bed was swollen and miserable. He was awake and in a great deal of pain.

"Hello friend," Johnny whispered, as he approached the bed.

"Do I know you?" the suffering man inquired.

"No you don't, but I have a lot of the same friends you have on the United Shows. I just came in to see about you. By the way, my name is Johnny Palmer. What's yours?"

"Bill Cash," came the reply.

"Is there anything I can do for you?" Johnny inquired, as he shook Bill's hand.

"After this afternoon," Bill said, "I didn't think I had a friend within a hundred miles of here. I need to

With It—For It—and Up Against It

let the Schaffers (owners of United Shows) know what happened and where I'm at," he said thoughtfully.

Johnny sensed the dread and loneliness of the injured man and said, "I can handle that. I don't suppose you have a phone number where they can be reached?" he asked kindly, as he searched himself for a pen and paper.

Bill's face seemed to light up as he recited the number. "I can't tell you how grateful I am for your assistance. I've been laying here all night trying to figure out how I was going to get word to the Schaffers. I knew eventually they'd find me but until then," his voice trailed off as he seemed unsure what to say next.

"What does the doctor say about your condition, Bill? I know they'll want to know."

The air seemed to fill with tension as Bill sighed in a loud melancholy way and said, "As near as I can tell I'm going to be here until the swelling in my head goes down. They say they're watching for any ill affects from the concussion. Up 'til now they have been very pleased. I'm a lucky man. I won't pull a stunt like this ever again. The Schaffers knew nothing of my unethical plan," he continued. "They would never have allowed me to raid another show for ride help! On top of everything else, I've probably lost my job. I was desperate. I know now I must have been off my rocker to devise such a plan. None the less, here I am," Bill admitted, as Johnny prepared to leave.

Johnny left the room promising to call the Schaffers at a reasonable hour that same morning.

Returning to the waiting room he found Happy awake and hungry. "It's about time for the cafeteria to open," Happy announced with a big grin. "You're gonna buy me a big breakfast and I'm going to tell you some great news," Happy promised.

Happy and Johnny were first in line as the cafeteria doors opened for business. Little was said as they filled their trays. Finding a table by the window they proceeded to knock the edge off their hunger pangs. It had been a long night. The food quietly disappeared. Happy returned with a second cup of coffee for both of them.

"Johnny, Greta and I are getting married next week," he announced, as he set the coffee down on the table.

"Son, you didn't waste any time, did you?" Johnny declared, as he sipped his coffee quietly.

Happy laughed and said, "I told you she was the one. If I can keep her mesmerized a few more days I'll close the deal. I would have asked you to be my best man, but I knew it would be a real hardship. You can't stop the carnival just because I'm getting hitched."

Johnny agreed with good natured humor and said, "I guess congratulations are in order. Here we are in a hospital, in less than ideal circumstances and as usual you come up with some happy news. How do you do it?" Johnny asked in a bewildered tone.

Happy's face suddenly grew serious as he informed Johnny that all the details had not been completely covered. "I still haven't secured the blessing of the Lomillers. I'm not sure how they are going to react." Happy coolly stated, "I tell you one thing for sure, Greta and I are going to be married."

"Take it easy!" Johnny instructed. "These things have a way of working out. I'm sure by now they have an idea what your plans are. They aren't blind or stupid. They may not know much about you, but they know a lot about their own daughter. If she hasn't told them, her brother has. If not, she's set them up for you to tell them," he continued, as he set his empty coffee cup down.

"You know as well as I do that they're good people," Johnny declared sincerely. "They just haven't been exposed to anyone like you before. Remember now, your future wife nicknamed you picture boy. Not every body's son-in-law is covered from head to toe with tattoos."

"Johnny, I'm not trying to be unreasonable," Happy said agreeably. "I just want you to know how strongly I feel about Greta. I'm aware of the reactions people have when they first see me. I spent a few years observing their faces, as they viewed me as a freak in the sideshow. Somehow, her parents are going to have to get past my altered appearance. I intend to give their daughter the best of everything," Happy promised.

"Whoa, big fella!" Johnny said, as he raised his hands in surrender. "Don't tell me. Tell them. I already believe in you. They need to hear what you just told me," he counseled. "Remember, they want what you want. They want Greta to be happy. In your case you want Greta to be happy, with Happy," Johnny said wisely, as a smile flashed across his face.

With It—For It—and Up Against It

"What say we head back to the waiting room? Maybe they've located Popsicle's problem," Johnny said hopefully, as they picked up their trays and headed toward the exit.

The waiting room had once again filled with descriptive faces. Some were new, some were now familiar. The doctors were making their rounds. Johnny and Happy were optimistically waiting with the rest of the concerned families and friends. They wouldn't have to wait long.

"Johnny Palmer," the doctor sounded out, as he entered the waiting room. Johnny responded by lifting his hand and moving toward the doctor. With clipped tones, precise and to the point, the doctor informed them of Popsicle's condition.

"Your friend is very lucky or real hardheaded, I don't know which. He is awake and we expect him to recover completely," the doctor stated with confidence. "The outcome in cases like his is not always so optimistic. He'll be here a couple of days, by then he should be able to leave," the doctor ventured.

"Doc, what do you suppose he was beaten with?" Johnny asked.

Rubbing his tired eyes, the doctor speculated, "He received a number of blows to the head. I would estimate some kind of weapon was used, extremely hard, quite deadly. I don't foresee any side effects or future complications. Again, he's a lucky individual."

"When can we see him?" Johnny asked.

"I should think now might be as good a time as any. If you have no further questions, I'll check

With It—For It—and Up Against It

on him again tonight," the doctor promised, as he quickly walked down the corridor.

Johnny and Happy walked down to the nurse's station and discovered Popsicle's Room 457 was right next door to the ride superintendent from United Shows. Johnny opened the door a little and peaked inside. Immediately, Popsicle waved him into the room. You could tell he was glad to see both Johnny and Happy. "Come in boys and take a look at the biggest fool in this city," Popsicle said seriously, as he reached for a cigarette.

Striking a match he lit a Lucky, inhaled deeply and sank back in the pillows. "You look a lot better than you did a few hours ago," Happy declared, as he walked up beside the bed.

Before Johnny could speak, Popsicle said, "Boss, I'm truly sorry for this mess. I know I brought it on myself. Seems like every once in a while I gotta throw a shoe and get drunk. I don't blame you if you fire me! I'm hoping you'll give me another chance."

"You just get well," Johnny advised. "You'll have a job. I'm sorry this has happened to you. Maybe it's a wake-up call that you'll hear and heed. We all make mistakes. Trouble is, with you it almost cost you your life."

Johnny's face flashed dark and threatening, as he asked, "One other thing more Popsicle, do you know who jumped you?"

"Boss, I haven't got a clue," Popsicle replied doubtfully. "I remember being in the G top and little else. I think, at one time, I had won a lot of money but I can't prove it now!" After a few minutes of small talk it was time to leave. Popsicle seemed to tire very quickly.

"Tell you what," Johnny said abruptly, as they walked toward the door, "you try to relax and get well, and we'll go through this later. Happy and I need to get back to the lot. I'll check on you some time this evening. If you need anything, have them call the Wright Show's office."

Popsicle said goodbye to his friends as they left the room. He felt a great relief that Johnny had been so forgiving. *That's the best medicine I've had all night,* he thought as a happy smile crossed his swollen face.

Arriving back at the carnival lot, Johnny and Happy walked in the cookhouse. As soon as they arrived, quite a number of concerned carneys, including Shorty Yeager, crowded around them.

Johnny informed them of Popsicle's condition, and the optimistic prognosis of the doctor. Other questions were asked pertaining to the identity of the assailant, to which there was no definitive answer.

"Johnny, we can all celebrate tonight!" Bill Charity exclaimed. "Popsicle is going to be alright and all my kitchen help is back at work, sober and sorry. Life ain't all bad," he celebrated, as he kicked up a little sawdust.

Remembering his promise to Bill Cash, Johnny left Happy at the cookhouse and walked toward the pay phone booths located under the grandstand. He then placed his call with the long distance phone operator. Upon reaching the United Show office, the manager took down the information pertaining to

With It—For It—and Up Against It

the whereabouts and condition of their ride superintendent. Having completed his promise, he looked forward to a shower and a shave as he headed toward his trailer.

The day passed quickly and night settled in friendly and full of promise. The midway magically came alive with colored lights and enticing sounds.

Down in the back end of the midway, the first evening presentation of owner Slick Maller's highly touted burlesque show was about to begin. His nickname best described his suave, scintillating presence on stage.

Born and bred in Miami Beach, he personified an understated elegance. He was smooth, could talk a Quaker preacher into being a fighter pilot. Slick was always attired in custom-made silk shirts and high dollar tropical suits that seemed to intensify his dark golden tan and boyish good looks. He was a startling contrast to the usual rough and raw bump and grind girl show operator. With care and confidence, he begins his fascinating spell binding enticements.

"Gonna be all free right down here in front of the Midnight Revue!" Slick Maller promised. "Gonna bring out the girl with the green hair! It's midnight ramble time! Gonna be all free! Girls! Girls! Girls! Here at the Midnight Revue."

The trombone inspired music, Night Train, was blaring hot and rhythmic out of two loudspeaker horns. The beautifully and scantly clad burlesque beauties walk on the bally stage like fashion models

With It—For It—and Up Against It

on a runway. Tall and erect, gliding to the sensual sounds of the music, they take their positions, two on each side as they undulate and rotate to the delight of the audience.

With dramatic impact, Vanilla Sugar appears center stage. Seductively she gyrates with a minimum of movement. Immediately, all eyes are drawn to her. Young and old are infatuated by her presence and appearance.

Her exquisite figure and creamy white skin is exposed in an alluring evening gown that reveals her ample assets and yet leaves just enough undisclosed to incite the imagination.

Slick Maller points out into the audience and promises, "Ladies and gentleman, it's burlesque, the way you like it! Naughty, but nice! Risqué and revealing! Red hot and entertaining! Ladies, it's even educational! We'll teach you how to keep your husband home on Saturday night without baking a cake! It's so red hot, no one under the age of eighteen will be admitted!"

Slick previews the daring dances to be performed inside with embellished descriptions hot enough to melt an Alaskan igloo.

With perfect timing he turns the attention of the audience to the ticket boxes on each side and declares, "The show starts in three minutes!"

The sultry sounds of the trombone cue the dancers to exit center stage as Slick informs the mesmerized throng, "You won't have to wait, but you will have to hurry! It's show time, at the Midnight Revue! There are tickets available on each side of the platform.

You're just in time to get in line. Just starting! Just commencing! Show time, at the Midnight Revue!"

The ensnared and excited sweep up to the ticket boxes and into the tent, like lost sheep ready to be sheared.

CHAPTER EIGHT

༄

Malcolm picked up his phone and listened, as the caller on the other end of the line identified himself. "Malcolm, this is H. L. Shaffer. I'm calling to apologize for the ruckus my ride superintendent initiated yesterday." H. L. went on to explain, "I had nothing to do with his plot to hire your ride help."

Malcolm, wishing to assure him said, "I never for a moment, thought you did H. L., anymore than I had anything to do with Pollock's brutal assault on your man," he stated, as he watched Dixie walk in the office and take a seat on the couch.

"Well, he asked for it," H. L. remarked. "What can I do to square things?"

"H. L., you don't owe me a thing," Malcolm answered. "We're friends, and I value your friendship. I'm certainly glad you called, and as for yesterday, it's over and done with. Let's just forget it."

"I tell you what, Malcolm," he replied. "You've been real decent about this matter and I won't forget

With It — For It — and Up Against It

it," he continued. "I'll look forward to seeing you at the showman's convention this fall. There are a couple of deals I plan to include you in. Give my regards to your lovely wife. Call me if I can help you in any way," H. L. said, as he hung up the phone.

"Was that H. L. Shaffer?" Dixie inquired.

"The very one," Malcolm answered. "It looks like that little skirmish yesterday is going to turn out for our good," he declared.

Dixie had been surprised lately at Malcolm's behavior. He had been so positive and upbeat – and he had been sober. She wasn't sure what had happened to him. Whatever it was, she hoped it continued.

Malcolm immediately noticed how good she looked. It dawned on him, he really hadn't taken notice of her in a long, long time. Another of his senses was awakened as he sat down next to her. She smelled like heaven on earth.

"My Lord Dixie, you look and smell wonderful," he said, as he moved closer to her.

She didn't know what to say or think. Malcolm hadn't said anything kind or considerate to her in ages. She felt the blush of excitement flash across her face. Good gracious, she thought, I'm acting like a schoolgirl.

"I'm so glad you came in Dixie, there's something I've been wanting to discuss with you," Malcolm said softly. "I've been waiting to get my courage up. I've been searching for the right moment. I believe this is it."

Dixie couldn't imagine what was about to transpire. One thing was certain, things couldn't get much worse than they already were. She could feel her pulse pounding as her heart beat at a rapid pace. Her breath was coming in short gasps. She was thoroughly curious and apprehensive at the same time. Somehow, she knew their future together was about to be decided in the next few minutes.

"Dixie, first of all, I want to ask you to forgive me for these last few years. I have been a terrible detriment to your happiness, as a husband and as a person, I've failed you miserably."

Malcolm took a deep breath and continued. "It started at the trial. From there, bad thoughts and booze consumed me. I've been a self-absorbed fool. I would love to spend the rest of my life caring for you and loving you. I'm asking you for a second chance," he said carefully, as he searched her face intently.

Dixie couldn't believe her ears. I must be dreaming, she thought. This isn't happening. In a moment I will awaken and discover, it's only make believe. He's not here and I'm not hearing what I'm hearing, she mused, as she wondered about her own sanity. Suddenly, she felt all hot and sweaty. From far off she could hear her name being called. Someone's arms were holding her tenderly. She was unaware she had fainted.

Malcolm called her name again and again, "Dixie! Dixie! Honey, can you hear me? Are you all right? Please answer me if you can." Troubled at her lack of response, he laid her head down carefully. He quickly opened a cabinet and found a towel, wet it and laid it on her forehead. He was about to summon some of the office help from the next room when she regained consciousness.

With her head still swimming, she attempted to sit up, only to discover her body would not respond. Malcolm thoughtfully encouraged her to remain in a prone position. She couldn't help but notice he looked like a frightened schoolboy. With a worried tone Malcolm said, "Just take it easy. You fainted. Would you like a cold drink or perhaps a little brandy?"

She could feel her adrenaline rushing to her rescue. Already she felt improved. Her strength was returning and she could focus her eyes properly. In a few more moments she would be able to sit up.

"I'm fine, Malcolm," Dixie said as she sat upright. "I guess I'm not used to this kind of treatment. Sorta threw me for a loop," she allowed, as she smiled pleasantly at him.

"You better get prepared," Malcolm advised. "I've got some news you're gonna find hard to believe."

"How much of that brandy do you have?" she asked teasingly. "You already have my heart fluttering and my mind faltering. I'm not even sure I'm awake," she admitted in astonishment.

"Dixie, do you remember when we met there in Las Vegas? Do you recall how unsure and nervous I was? Well, I'm more shaky than that now!" he admitted hesitantly.

Malcolm stood as tall as his slight stature would allow, took a deep breath and said, "The only thing I know to do is just say it. Dixie, I got saved! I've been born again! I made Jesus the Lord of my life," he declared dramatically. "I'm a changed man. I'm off the gin. I'm hoping we can start anew."

Dixie didn't know whether to laugh or cry. This was the one thing she would have never thought of — Malcolm Wright a Christian. "Don't that just beat all," she thought, as she realized she had just quoted her Mother's favorite saying.

Without waiting, hoping to help his cause, Malcolm proceeded to unveil his story of redemption. Dixie sat transfixed as the words rushed out of his mouth. It was as though a pent up dam had burst.

When he had finished, he was bewildered to discover both of them were weeping. He had no knowledge of his own torrent of tears until he discovered his shirt was damp with saltine brine.

Dixie wiped the tears from her eyes and realized she had just witnessed an unforeseen union of God and man. Malcolm was a living demonstration of the unparalleled grace of a loving God. He was changed, that was undeniable.

She felt ashamed of her indiscriminate behavior. She had never loved anyone but Malcolm. Until now, the prospect of being reconciled had seemed impossible. If anything, she felt she was the one who needed to be forgiven.

"Oh Malcolm," Dixie said as she struggled to gain her composure. "Of course, I'll forgive you, but only if you will forgive me. I've been both terrible and thoughtless."

Before she could divulge her unfaithful acts, Malcolm interrupted her and insisted. "We are not going to dig up the past. I don't want to know what may have happened. What's important, is what we do from here on," he kindly stated as he approached Dixie, who was still seated on the couch.

"There's so much I want to tell you," he said in an inclusive manner, as he sat next to her. "If every thing works out, I was hoping we could start a family," he informed her with suppressed excitement.

Dixie turned toward him in enthusiastic joy, nodding her head in full agreement. It was all the encouragement Malcolm needed. He held her possessively and embraced her with emblazoned passion. It was a moment locked in time, bearing the seal of heaven's approval.

Dixie, in a long contented sigh of sufficiency thought, dreams really do come true, as they held each other tightly. They were so happy and so relieved to once more be in love.

With her face beaming with anticipation and relief, Dixie ventured in a seductive tone. "Why don't we go downtown, rent a nice suite of rooms and initiate our plan for more Wrights and less wrongs?" she said, grinning with the impetuous smile of a young bride. "With just a few arrangements, there is no reason not to," Malcolm replied, as he squeezed Dixie's hand.

"One other thing Malcolm, do you think Silvia would mind telling me how to be saved?" Dixie innocently asked.

Malcolm's heart was singing as he quickly replied, "I'm sure she wouldn't mind darling. We'll do that first thing. That is, almost first thing," he said, as his face flashed a tinge of red.

Time passed quickly and Sunday arrived. Tonight was slough night. Popsicle had been released from the hospital and had taken his familiar post at the cork gallery. Up and down the midway preparations were being made for tonight's tear down.

Happy walked in the cookhouse and sat down at a table where Johnny, Agatin Bill and Slick Maller were sitting. As he was about to initiate some lively conversation, Pollock came striding in the cookhouse. His face was livid with anger. He ignored everyone and took a table at the back of the cookhouse. Surly and mean he barked out his order.

Watching Pollock's uncivil entrance and subsequent mistreatment of the waiter infuriated Slick Maller. His eyes narrowed to tiny slits, he gritted his teeth and said, "I should of shot that bastard in the G top when I had the chance." Until now, Johnny had not learned the identity of the individual who had come to the rescue of his battered agent. Now, he knew.

Pollock's fierce countenance was the result of some recently acquired information from Shorty Yeager. The reconciliation of Dixie and Malcolm and their abbreviated honeymoon had ignited his vile temper. "Who did she think she was?" he mumbled, as he vigorously stirred his coffee. "Nobody treats me like trash and gets by with it," he fumed, as the waiter carefully set his sandwich down in front of him and scurried away.

With It—For It—and Up Against It

Clinching his jaw, his mood darkened even further when he saw Johnny, Happy and Slick. Maybe it was time to find out just how game Johnny Palmer was, he thought sullenly, as he tore at his sandwich.

All the soreness had left his hands. A lot quicker than Bill Cash's face, he reminded himself wickedly, as he considered his next move. What would it take to get Palmer going? All I need is an excuse, he thought. I've been aching to bust up that pretty boy face. "Now might be a good time," he said to himself, as he deliberated the possibilities.

"Slick, I owe you one," Johnny declared, as he got up to leave. "I won't forget what you did for my agent," he promised.

"Forget it," Slick replied. "You would have done the same for me," he said, as a knowing grin flashed across his face.

"What's your hurry?" Happy asked, as Johnny turned to leave. "Let's just say, today is not the day I settle my account with Pollock. He's way to testy for me to hang around," Johnny advised, as he walked out of the cookhouse.

Pollock was even more angry when he realized his opportunity to challenge Johnny had disappeared. He looked at Happy and Slick, but he knew Slick was always packing a .38. He was mad, but he wasn't that mad.

"Gimme another cup of coffee," Pollock demanded, as Happy and Slick walked out on the midway.

The sun had set and once again the gleaming colors of the midway beamed with vivid, luminous refraction's of light. The crowd seemed to be in a frenzied spending mode. The last few hours were all that remained of this year's fair. They surged up and down the midway, attempting to pursue as many thrills and as much excitement as was humanly possible in the allotted time that was left. It had been a record-breaking day. The mesmerized throng began to dwindle somewhere around eleven o'clock.

All kinds of emotions had been aroused as they hastened toward the parking lot. Many were excited and astounded as they carried their treasured teddy bears and carnival treats. Others were agitated and angry, bristling at their own stupidity, nothing in their hands and nothing in their wallets.

All will be back next year, a few a little wiser. A great many will come longing to beat the carneys at their own game. Carrying enough cash to further their education.

Thankfully, for the carnival, they are a year off from being wise. Consequently, there's a new crop every year. The great showman P.T. Barnum was right. There is a sucker born every minute.

The next few weeks passed quickly as summer intruded into fall. The citics and states hosting the fairs were located further and further south.

School had started and the opening calls of the carnival had been moved from morning to afternoon, except Saturdays and Sundays.

Most calls were set for two o'clock during the week. It gave the carneys a little more rest, but posed the problem of keeping an annoying number of them

With It—For It—and Up Against It

sober. It seems some carneys can handle about everything except an abundance of free time.

After the show closed on the opening day of the first state fair on the southern schedule, the differences in southern and northern cultures were about to be emphasized with force.

Dr. Dubious had contracted to travel with the Mighty Wright Shows for three weeks. The fairs had been so profitable he decided to stay on through the southern route.

John Wesley, who worked for Dr. Dubious, had found some drinking buddies down at the Harlem Hot Spot. On the northern route it had been a top moneymaker. It was burlesque at its best, with an all-black cast. Many of the members of the show had never been this far south.

As the uninhibited party got in to full swing it seemed to accumulate an ever-increasing number of participants. Before long, some of the members of the band were making music, hot and loud. Others were dancing. It was a rambunctious crowd. Booze and drugs were fueling their bouts of ecstasy. Their drug-induced joy would be short lived.

The following morning, the old hands were out early searching for money under the shake rides and other items dropped on the midway. It was one of them who discovered the declaration of depraved despotism inscribed on the burnt-out cross, KKK.

The cross, in the early morning light, looked like an article from outer space. Even now it was large and imposing, exceeding eight feet. Its burnt-out timbers reached toward heaven as though it was seeking reassurance from God for its calamitous conspiracy. Its crosspiece spread its charred arms in a forced embrace, declaring its sickened aversion to the assassin's symbol carved in its wood. The symbol of righteousness perverted, reduced to an instrument of malicious hate and malevolent destruction, disturbed and depraved, the creation of an inflamed diabolical brotherhood.

When Johnny arrived at the backend of the midway, a large crowd of carneys had already assembled. John Wesley was giving his recollections of the previous night to Noble Fairly. Many of the cast, fearing for their lives, had left everything and fled in the night.

The grand wizard who spoke for the robed and hooded Klan had promised a return visit if the black burlesque show dared to pursue business in this particular county.

One of the things carneys do not respond kindly to, is threats, veiled or otherwise. They prize their independence. They were not about to allow anyone from outside to come in and dictate when and how members of the carnival would operate.

Those of the black cast that remained were assured that the entire population of the carnival was committed to protecting their safety and independence at all costs. It was certain the local authorities weren't going to get involved. Who knew, it could be that some of them were a part of last night's dastardly act.

For many of the carneys the only family and home they had was the midway. It would be a perilous act to enter their domain with thoughts of exercising your will to rule and regulate.

A blood bath was brewing and many on the midway were looking forward to inflicting judgement, malicious and methodical — practiced portions of punishment that had been tested and tried. Fiercely competitive, they were unaccustomed to failure.

It's an appropriate act to question the wisdom and sanity of anyone or any group who came looking for trouble on a carnival midway. The rules of conflict include claw hammers, tent stakes, sledgehammer handles and anything hard, handy and advantageous. After all, this is not the YMCA.

The day passed and the night was inhabited with deliberations of response and speculations of force. Would the Klan make good their threat? If so, when? What were they willing to sacrifice to claim victory?

If they came, the cowardly bunch of terrorists was about to enter some unexplored territory. They had never engaged an army of enraged carneys. Once tried, they would never do it again, that was certain.

The carneys were confident of the outcome. For one thing this wasn't their first confrontation with a mob. As to their commitment, the carnival lot was their home.

The most important aspect of any conflict is, what will you expend to win. You must be willing. They were almost fanatical in their desire to defend the lot and those who live and work on it.

If the hooded bullies came, the sawdust trail would run red with blood. Uncontrollable fury was about to be unleashed. Caution and compassion would find no consideration among the carneys. A deposit of pain and misery was about to be made in the bank vault of anguish and despair.

The Harlem Hot Spot opened that night with less than half of the original cast. The usually sensual and seductive dancers appeared on stage, constrained and concerned, looking about as though they were searching for a friendly face among their white-skinned patrons.

There was no doubt they were frightened. Who wouldn't be? The night air heavy with humidity seemed to support the stifling alarm and sickening dread emanating from the platform.

They would be required to go through this process of fear and fright for the next three days. Each day the threat became less terrifying, their vigil less intense, their hope of security more wistful and speculative. Maybe it was over. Everyone pondered the possibility. No one believed it.

Every mark, in every city in America, believes that the call to fight for carneys is preceded by the phrase "Hey Rube". Johnny Palmer had been with the carnival all his life and had never heard those words. He didn't know, perhaps the former generation had signaled their cohorts with this peculiar call, but he doubted it.

On that ominous Friday night, a little past midnight, the Klan came. As if by magic the carneys in large number appeared. They arrived armed with claw hammers, two-by-fours, and other objects of enforcement, plus an abundance of bad attitudes.

With It—For It—and Up Against It

Embracing the opportunity to exercise their pent up wrath they surged forward. No one wanted to be last. On the Klan side, no one wanted to be first. Many of those who had come had been pressured or shamed to fill their ranks.

One of the leaders of the intruders, sadly lacking in understanding regarding the rules of engagement, decided a speech punctuated with profanity was in order. It was his intention to lecture the carneys on the dangers of offending the Klan by reopening the Hot Spot Revue.

He scarcely got out three cuss words when the carneys rushed in with murderous fury. They had no intention in participating in some ineffectual debate. Frenzied recklessness has no reason, only madness intent upon revenge.

The next forty seconds would require a half a dozen ambulances piled high with disabled trespassers, an ample supply of blood and emergency staff numerous enough to care for the brutalized intruders.

Some were suffering with broken bones. Others broken in spirit had run away in terror. It was nothing like they had planned.

The battered and bloody Klansmen were outnumbered and outfought. Shocked and traumatized, they were unaccustomed to being punished for their belligerent behavior. Many would bear the scars of that night for the rest of their lives.

The aftermath looked like a war zone. Many of the carneys were covered in their victim's blood.

With It—For It—and Up Against It

Few, if any had suffered injuries or wounds. It had been an unfair fight. That's as it was suppose to be.

This confrontation had come about not because the carneys opposed the Klan. Some of their own number may have been Klansman at one time. They could have cared less what the Klan did as long as it didn't include them.

It was not a fight for integration. The carnival philosophy of life made room for everyone regardless of race or color. It was already integrated. If you would work like a mule, fight like a bear and mind your own business they didn't care what color you were.

The rule of conflict for carneys is short and simple. Win at any cost, in any way necessary. Their mission accomplished; there would be little celebration and even less talk tomorrow. Their self-image was not captive to declarations of victory. Next week the challenges of life will compel them to solve another kind of dilemma. It was the price you pay for a life unfettered by conformity. It wasn't near as bad as you might suppose. Many would testify to its beguiling, mesmerizing influence that made the heart soar.

CHAPTER NINE

Next morning, Noble Fairly was up early, fielding the many questions, accusations and insinuations leveled by the local authorities. The incendiary violence of the previous night had tinctured the city father's thinking with alarm and fear of exposure. Their hope of exoneration depended on their plot to successfully disengage themselves from any knowledge of the violence or any of its participants.

One justice of the peace, a county commissioner and a number of prominent community leaders, who served on the board of some of the cities most prestigious churches, were in the hospital with maimed and mauled body parts. The broken bones and swollen heads of their compatriots, recovering in rooms nearby, testified to the widespread success of the carneys.

Because of the nature of the conflict and the notoriety of the participants, who were as anxious as the carnival to silence any adverse publicity, nothing was printed in the local paper. Their motivation for silence was predicated on the preservation of their good name and their social standing in the community. The carneys only wish was to prevent any loss of revenue. Money was the issue; nothing else mattered.

Noble listened with the practiced ear of a diplomat as the politicians and city fathers vehemently harped on the carneys disgraceful attack on their upstanding citizens. They conveniently excused the Klan, declaring them to be innocent bystanders who just happened to be present during the carneys evil and unscrupulous assault.

After they had emptied themselves of their supplications of delusion and fraud, the lush wagon would be their next stop. With hands extended, palms turned upward, money would ultimately silence their declarations of outrage.

Noble sat alone in the lush wagon after the local dignitaries had drunk their fill, pocketed their pieces of silver and self-righteously returned to their constituents. He was hard pressed to tell who the crooks were and who the civic-minded citizens were. As near as he could tell a permanent address was the only difference.

His mind wandered back to his early days as a defense attorney in good standing. Taking a big pull on a glass filled with three fingers of scotch, he remembered his disbarment. It had come about as a result of an ambitious member of the law firm. An unscrupulous attorney framed him in an effort to eliminate competition. He had done this to insure

With It — For It — and Up Against It

Noble would not impede his own ascension to the top of the firm.

Noble had been celebrated as the most proficient defense attorney on the East Coast. His ability as a spellbinder and mesmerizer was well earned. His presence and personality would fill any courtroom and often overpower the members of the jury. His winning ways in behalf of some of America's most prominent people had gained him national notoriety.

The charges leveled against him were ridiculous. Members of his own staff, who had been promised promotions as a reward for their false testimony, had conspired to effect his downfall. The charge was jury tampering. Not only was it untrue, it was unnecessary. Everyone connected with the case seemed to have left reason and common sense outside the courtroom.

Nobel's day in court revealed America's justice was not only blind, but also ensconced in betrayal. His reputation had been stolen and savaged in the courtroom of corruption and dishonor. His fellow barristers were certain the charges against him were false. Their absence in court belied their belief and sealed his doom.

Noble shook his head as if he was trying to erase the images and inaccuracies of that calamitous day — twenty-four hours that had expressed itself in cruelty and ruthlessness — betrayed and banished from the confines of the courtroom that had witnessed some of his greatest triumphs.

His vociferous outcry had fallen on felonious ears. The judge and his paid conspirators were unwilling to hear. The long arm of the law had been shortened to the length of a small man's ambitions.

Lost in thought, Noble was unaware of Willie's approach. Willie was surprised when he walked into the lush wagon and discovered Noble, sitting alone at the bar. The office manager had informed him that the electrical outlets behind the bar were inoperable and he had picked this particular time to fix it.

"Oh, hello Willie." Noble wasn't in the mood for company. "What brings you to this wagon of bottled and bonded joy?" he asked, finishing his drink. Willie walked behind the bar and started examining the electrical outlets before he replied to Noble's question. "Well sir," Willie said, a big grin spreading across his dark face, revealing a pair of gold-capped front teeth, "I've come to fix whatever is broke. That includes you, from the looks of your face."

Noble laughed out loud, realizing how perceptive Willie's offer of aid was. He poured himself another drink and declared, "If it were possible, I just bet you could fix me. Sadly, what ails me has found no solution in the passing of more than a few years," Noble continued. "Don't think I'm not grateful for the offer, because I am," he stated, watching Willie's skillful hands continued to work.

"Can I ask you something?" Willie ventured, as he opened the circuit breaker box and turned it off. "Are you going to be able to get the rest of the Hot Spot members and cast to return to the lot?"

Noble reached in the humidor for a Cuban cigar and replied, "If we can locate them, we are certainly gonna try to. God only knows how far north they fled, not that I blame them. Hell, I'd still be going," Noble admitted, lighting the hand-rolled Monte Cristo.

As Willie continued to work his particular brand of magic on the electrical outlets, Noble decided to satisfy the curiosity he had harbored these many weeks regarding the death of the man found under the tilt trailer. "Tell me something, Willie, what really happened to that bruised and battered body Snag Hughes ran over?"

Willie rose from the floor, slow and impassive, his eyes against his dark skin seemed even whiter than usual as they widened and looked cautiously at Noble. "Why you wanna ask me that?" Willie inquired softly, searching Noble's face for an answer.

"Don't misunderstand me," Noble reassured him. "I'm not reopening the case. I'm just interested in what really took place. I did a background check on that fellow and discovered he was a repeat sex offender. He'd done time in the state pen for molesting little children. Everyone in his hometown seemed glad that he was no longer among the living."

Moving back to the circuit breaker box, Willie flipped the switch back on and said, "Sounds to me like it don't much matter who done what. It's for certain he was too wretched to live. Man like that's like a snake, the quicker you stomp his head, the better. Whoever shortened his length of days deserves our gratitude," Willie said thoughtfully, as he checked the outlet and grunted in satisfied approval.

"Well, looks like I've done it again. Everything is repaired and ready to go," Willie said, as he waved a pretended magic wand. "I'll tell you this, Noble,"

Willie said seriously heading toward the door, "you just take my word for it, that sack of trash bagged up and laying under Snag's tilt trailer got exactly what he had coming." The door shut silently behind Willie as he descended the stairs and walked out on the midway.

"And that's that," Noble said out loud, finishing his drink. It wasn't necessary to explore the events leading up to the sex offender's death any further. He had a defense lawyer's intuition into what had transpired. He wasn't far from the truth and he knew it. Might as well go get a cup of coffee, he decided, easing out of the trailer, locking the door behind him.

Dixie was excited about the morning's activities. Silvia had invited her to a prayer meeting at the Brown's trailer. She didn't know what to expect, but she was sure of one thing, it would be a blessing.

So much about her had changed since she surrendered her life to Jesus. Silvia had been most kind and helpful in furthering her understanding of Jesus and his Word.

Lost in thought, she was unaware of her surroundings as she walked behind a row of joints. Intent on locating Silvia's trailer, she turned a corner and came face to face with Pollock.

"Well, well, well, if it ain't the Virgin Mary herself," Pollock said sarcastically. Dixie attempted to walk around him but he quickly blocked her approach. Pollock's large body loomed over her tiny stature like a cloud of impending doom. His face animated with confident fury darkened in delight at the prospect of exacting his pound of flesh. He would have his revenge. She would suffer as he had suffered. He would see to that.

He leered at her, inquiring, "Where have you been, love eyes? I haven't been able to find you for weeks. You been too busy for old lover boy, have you?" Pollock sneered, grabbing her wrists.

Dixie struggled to free herself from Pollock's vice-like grip. "You would be wise to leave me alone," she said forcefully. "You and I are history. Let's just leave it at that," she said coolly, attempting to free herself.

"You don't get off that easy," he snarled, holding her hostage. "You're gonna pay for your low-down cheatin' ways. I'll see to that," he promised, glaring hatefully at her, eyes sullen and dangerous. "Maybe I'll just stuff you in one of these possum bellies and take what's coming to me. I've lived like a Priest these past few weeks. You owe me! I'm thinking now's as good a time as any to collect. Right now is good for me," he declared, as he dragged Dixie toward one of the semi-trailers.

She attempted to scream but Pollock roughly covered her mouth with his huge hand. "You might as well cooperate. It's not like it's your first time," Pollock stated with unrelenting vengeance. "Would you like to confess you sins to Father Pollock?" he mocked insultingly, savagely flinging her into the trailer storage compartment.

Dixie felt the bottom of the compartment scrape her back as he slammed her to the floor. The pain was like a fire flickering up and down her spine. Her attempts to scream only intensified the pain. Her head swimming, she fought valiantly to remain conscious.

Pollock's face looked more like an animal than a man. His demented mind had forsaken any thoughts of mercy or sanity. The howling sounds of demonic glee roared in his ears. His body language signaled his frenzied intention to conquer and perhaps kill.

Fighting with all her might, Dixie's hand groping for anything to defend herself, found a small tent stake, cool to the touch and made of steel. She struggled to shift her weight to the most advantageous position and struck him with unbridled fury, again and again, many times, many, until he lay upon her motionless. Blood was spurting from holes gouged in a varied pattern of places on his head. The possum belly appeared to have been splashed with crimson color. The gruesome hue cried out in testimony against his insidious attack.

Dixie managed to disengage herself from her tormentor, grateful to stand once again on solid ground. She searched Pollock's face for signs of life. It was possible she had killed him. She wasn't sure and right now she didn't care. All she had in mind was escape. Franticly, she ran and ran until she arrived at the Brown's trailer. Her strength all but depleted, she banged as hard as she could on the door.

Silvia was alarmed at the loud rapping sound on the other side of her trailer door and was even more alarmed when she pulled back the curtain and saw Dixie's appearance. The moment the door opened Dixie rushed in. "My Lord Dixie, what has happened?" Silvia nervously asked. Distraught, disheveled and marred with black grimy dirt and covered in blood, Dixie sank to the couch and began to weep.

Unaware of what had just occurred, Silva did her best to comfort and console Dixie. Upon closer examination she could see that Dixie's blouse had been torn open and her skirt was ripped. The backside of her blouse and skirt were also covered in black grime. The most telling foreign substance was what appeared to be bloodstains, crimson red, abundantly distributed. Her hair, face and clothing were covered in its rich red hue.

Dixie screamed hysterically, "I've killed him, God forgive me! I'm certain he's dead."

"Who is dead, Dixie?" Silva asked, trying to quiet her friend. "Try to calm yourself and tell me what I can do to help you," Silva spoke quietly holding on to Dixie who continued to tremble and shake.

"Pollock! I may have killed Pollock," she wailed, as she covering her face with her hands. Silvia was trying to figure out what on earth could have happened, how and where when the trailer door opened and Silvia's son, Dallas, stepped inside.

"Dixie, tell me where you left Pollock?" Silva requested loudly, hoping to break through her frantic sobbing. Dixie calmed herself enough to tell them where she had left him, crumpled and unconscious, perhaps dead.

Dallas bolted out the door and ran toward the semi trailers parked behind a row of joints. He searched trailer after trailer, but without any success. He was almost ready to give up when he discovered a red stained possum belly; the compartment was still soaked with blood. It looked like someone had slaughtered a hog in it, but Pollock was nowhere to be seen.

Unsure as to what to do, Dallas ran back to Silvia and Dixie. Arriving out of breath he blurted out, "He's not there! I found the trailer but he's not there!" he declared mystified, gasping for air.

Alarmed and even more afraid, Dixie asked, "What do you mean, he's not there? He's got to be there. Where else would he be?" she moaned, waving her hands emphasizing her plea for answers.

Silvia realized there was only one way to enable Dixie to gain control of her faculties and that was prayer. Silva and Dallas immediately began to pray and petition the Lord for guidance as Dixie wrung her hands and sobbed. "I've killed him! God, help me. I have killed him."

As the minutes passed, Silvia became more and more concerned about Dixie. Pale and now shivering as if the temperature had plunged forty degrees, Dixie continued to cry out to God. Silvia wrapped a light blanket around her, hoping to warm her body and silence the storm of emotions that chattered against her teeth. She then took a seat next to her on the couch, holding her as though she was a small child cradled in her arms, in an effort to console her. Dixie's mental anguish was such that Silva feared her tiny body might not hold up under the strain and shock of such intense anguish.

Silvia took the Bible from the end table and turned to Psalm 91. The Word of the Lord broke through Dixie's despair. The peace of God settled in the room, calming the quaking desperation of her soul. The ministering power of God's Holy Spirit comforted her and quieted her tumultuous emotions.

Dixie, realizing the extent of her actions, her face bloody and now swollen with grief and despair, moaned, "What am I going to tell Malcolm?" Stricken and uncertain, her agonized heart breaking, tears spilled down her face as she looked imploringly at Silvia.

"Dixie! Get hold of yourself," Silvia declared forcefully. "We don't know anything for sure. Think about it, if Pollock was dead then how come Dallas found the possum belly empty? There is a good chance he's alive," Silva said with certainty. "Let's get you cleaned up. That and a little rest will make you feel a lot better," Silva said, guiding Dixie toward the washroom.

"Oh Silvia, just when it looked like Malcolm and I were going to have a wonderful life together, this had to happen," Dixie sobbed, as she stood at the sink, her shoulders shaking.

Silvia spoke soothingly to Dixie, attempting to remove the blood that had saturated her hair and spotted her face. As Silvia continued her efforts to restore Dixie's appearance and placate her alarm, Dixie unburdened her soul and gave the details of Pollock's attack. Appalled at her actions of the present and the past, Dixie cried out, "God's punishing me for the terrible way I have lived. I wish I'd never been born," she wailed, once again seeming to lose her grip on reality.

"Dixie Wright, you listen to me," Silvia said, looking directly into Dixie's eyes. "God is a good God. He certainly didn't commission Pollock's attack on you. You think about this, you could have been killed. "When you were saved, when you were born again, did you ask God to forgive you of your sins? Well did you?" Silvia demanded.

"You know I did, Silvia, you were there when it happened," Dixie replied agreeably.

Silvia nodded her head and said, "Yes, I was there and yes, I heard you ask God to forgive you of your sins," Silvia continued. "The Bible says God hides our sins as far as the east is from the west. The Bible also says, once we confess our sins, God does not remember them anymore. We are declared not guilty. How could God punish you for something you have confessed and forsaken and he has forgotten?" Silvia asked, attempting to clean Dixie's hair.

Silvia turned toward Dallas who was waiting in the front of the trailer and said, "Dallas, I want you to find your father, tell him what's happened and see if you can find out anything about Pollock's condition."

"Momma, I'll come back the minute I know something," Dallas promised, hurrying out to find his father.

Dixie, with nerves frayed and spent, her body swaying and her head swimming, was close to collapsing. Sensing her trauma, Silvia guided her to the bedroom and assisted as Dixie crumpled onto the bed. Silva retrieved a cool cloth from the washroom and laid it on her head.

"There, there now, you're going to be alright," Silvia predicted, as Dixie once again began to shiver. Silva placed a warm quilt on her and the trembling and shivering subsided. She poured Dixie a full snifter of brandy. After consuming the generous serving, Dixie fell into a sedated sleep.

Silvia stayed by her side and pondered the startling episodes of the day. If Pollock was alive, where was he? Did someone move him? If so who? If not, how did he manage to disappear? Where did he go? These and other perplexing questions dominated her thinking.

"Lord," Silvia whispered softly, "please cause this mangled mess to work out for Dixie and Malcolm's good. Lord Jesus, I'm asking you to rescue them from the evil works of darkness. Deliver them from the snares of the flesh. Right every wrong. Heal every hurt, and dry every tear. I pray in the wonderful name of Jesus, Amen."

CHAPTER 10

At Pollock's demand, Shorty Yeager peered out of the window of Pollock's trailer, trying to see if any one had witnessed their arrival. Shorty had come upon Pollock staggering toward his trailer. He had been shocked to see the big Pollock so weakened and bloody and beaten. Supporting a portion of Pollock's weight, together they were able to negotiate the last few obstacles, stumbling and falling into the doorway of the trailer. After resting a few minutes, Shorty pulled and tugged at Pollock's big frame until he was able to drag him inside and shut the door.

It was obvious Pollock needed medical attention. Each time Shorty mentioned going for help, Pollock scalded his ears with life taking threats abundantly enhanced with the vilest of profanity. "You take one step out of this trailer and it'll take you a lifetime of living to get over it," Pollock snarled, as he struggled to get to his feet. "Now go back into the washroom and wet some towels and bring them here.

While you're back there, look in the medicine chest and bring me some aspirin. My head's killing me," Pollock complained, as he staggered toward a chair.

"I should have ignored the big bully," Shorty mumbled. "Who cares what happens to him. Let someone else find him. What do I care whether he lives or dies; it's not my problem. At least then I wouldn't have to suffer his ungrateful abuse," Shorty fumed, as he searched for the aspirin.

Pollock decided the best way to get rid of all the blood encrusted in his hair was to stick his head under the faucet in the kitchen sink. The cold water felt good to his throbbing head but each time he would rub his hand across his scalp the wounds would open and the blood would spurt more profusely.

Shorty returned with the towels and witnessed Pollock's attempt to free the numerous clots of blood from his hair. "Pollock," Shorty said with alarm, "you need some stitches, not only that, you need x-rays. You very likely have a concussion or worse. How are you going to stop all that bleeding, man? If you're not careful, you'll bleed to death!"

Pollock raised his head from the sink. The blood and water ran down his face. He opened a kitchen cabinet door, reached in and removed a half-full box of Arm and Hammer baking soda. "You pack ever one of these wounds with this baking soda," Pollock instructed, as he once again placed his head over the sink. Shorty did as he had been instructed. The only way he knew to pack the wounds was to pour the soda right out of the box on them, which is exactly what he did.

Pollock raised his head out of the sink and secured the towel around his head. Opening the cabinet door next to the refrigerator he wrapped his big hand around the neck of a fifth of Jack Daniel's. He set two water glasses down on the table and poured them both a drink. They needed it, Pollock for pain and Shorty for putting up with Pollock.

Pollock couldn't remember when he had ever felt so bad. He hurt all over. His head was pounding like it had been struck with a sledgehammer. His equilibrium had been affected. His head was swimming. He was unable to walk without staggering.

Shorty watched cautiously as Pollock lurched about the room. He emptied his glass of whiskey and wondered what would happen next.

Pollock looked at Shorty menacingly and said, "You don't know nothin'. You ain't seen nothin'. Do you get it?" Pollock asked. Shorty quickly replied, "I ain't seen nothin'. I don't know nothin'. I don't wonna know anything," he stated, looking nervously at the door.

Pollock moved away from the door. "If you tell anyone I'll rip your tongue out," he growled slow and mean, accomplishing his intention of acute intimidation. "Now get out of here! I got some serious drinking to do."

Shorty was out the door almost before Pollock finished his last sentence. "That's the thanks I get for helping," Shorty mumbled, as he walked toward the front gate. I wonder about those holes in his head. Where did Pollock come from? Who beat on his head and with what? Shorty was beside himself to know all the details. Being a cautious man, he was far more interested in staying alive and in one piece. With that in mind, he hightailed it to his own trailer and his own liquor.

Dallas found his father Don at the custard stand. He was finishing up cleaning the front glass and was climbing down the ladder.

Don looked at him and asked, "Where's the fire?"

Dallas, breathing rapidly replied, "Dad, Dixie's in trouble. Mom wants you to come to the trailer as quick as possible."

Don hurriedly placed the ladder inside the custard trailer, locked the side door and inquired, "What's happened son? Is it bad? Is your Mother alright?" Don asked. Questions and alarm swirled through his mind as they ran toward the trailer.

"Mom's fine," Dallas informed his father. "It's Dixie. She's in a terrible fix. I don't know many of the details. What I do know is this: She thinks she may have killed Pollock!"

Don could scarcely believe what he had just heard. How could something this disastrous occur now? Dixie and Malcolm had finally gotten their lives and marriage on track. Now this had to happen.

Arriving at the trailer, Don and Dallas rushed through the front door and were immediately met by Silvia. She quickly informed them of the need to lower their voices. "Dixie is asleep," Silva stated, as she squeezed Don's hand, so relieved and strengthened just by his presence.

For the next few minutes Silva rehearsed everything Dixie had told her. "Don, Dixie is determined to keep all of this from Malcolm if possible," Silva advised.

Don looked at her in amazement and said, "That may not be possible, especially if Pollock is dead or disabled. Malcolm will have to know," Don reasoned.

Silvia nodded her head in agreement and said seriously, "We'll cross that bridge when we come to it. Right now, we've got to get Dixie through these next few hours." Silvia, mindful of her own family looked at her husband and asked, "By the way Don, where's Pumpkin?"

Don paused a moment thinking, then said, "Oh yea, she's with Johnny. He had some stock shipped in by rail. They've gone to the depot to pick it up. She should be back within the hour," Don replied, as he got up from his chair, moved to the counter and poured himself a cup of coffee. Noticing that Dallas was anxious to leave, he nodded at him and said, "Son, go on back to the midway if you want to. I'm going to ask you not to say anything to anyone about what has happened here."

"Don't worry Dad, I'm not even sure I know what's happened. But if I did, I certainly wouldn't say anything because of Dixie," Dallas promised and he was out the door.

Out on the midway Pumpkin and Johnny had finished unloading the stock they had picked up at the railroad depot in town. Bennie was flashing the shelves of the cork gallery in preparation for another night of business.

Johnny looked approvingly at Bennie's work and said, "Bennie, you're a natural born artist. It looks so inviting, I may try to win one of those prizes myself," Johnny said grinning, as he and Pumpkin prepared to leave.

"How about you and I go find ourselves a cold drink?" Johnny asked Pumpkin.

Pumpkin smiled agreeably and took hold of his hand. With a woman's healthy curiosity Pumpkin asked, "How's Greta doing? Has she adjusted to life on the road? When are we going to get together?"

Pumpkin was about to fire another question at him. Before she could, he playfully interrupted her, "Slow down girl. I can only answer one question at a time." Johnny flashed a familiar smile. "Greta couldn't be any happier. She loves the road and is anxious to see you."

Pumpkin's face filled with delight. "Oh Johnny, I'm so happy everything is working out," Pumpkin said gleefully, as they approached the grandstand. "Why don't we try to get together with them after the show closes and have a meal?" Pumpkin continued her happy chatter. Johnny ordered tall cool lemon-lime drinks for them.

"Guess who's coming to visit in about two more weeks?" Johnny asked. Pumpkin paused for what seemed to him a long time, trying to imagine who it might be. "Do you give up?" he persisted, as she continued to search her mind for an answer.

Unwilling to wait any longer, he decided to tell her the good news and said, "Greta's parents, the Lomillers, are coming! They're all excited about discovering the untold truths about life on the carnival. Isn't that wonderful!" He watched Pumpkin's eyes widen in amazement.

Pumpkin could hardly contain her excitement. She looked searchingly at him. "You're not teasing me, are you Johnny? They really are coming! What brought about the big change?" Johnny blinked at her with exasperated emphasis, imitating her excited mannerisms.

"Picture boy has stolen their hearts." He paused to enjoy a long, refreshing drink.

Pumpkin was almost beside herself. "Well, go ahead, tell me what happened."

He knew that withholding the details of their alliance of friendship was tormenting Pumpkin to no end. Pumpkin pleaded, pulling on his arm like a small spoiled child, "Johnny Palmer, tell me what is going on."

Forcing himself to keep a straight face, Johnny told her all he knew. "Pumpkin, all I know is Happy said after the wedding was over they spent a few hours with Greta's parents and their animosity turned to admiration. They quickly learned that most of their preconceived ideas about carneys were incorrect."

Pumpkin snorted in a most unladylike fashion. "I guess they realized we really don't eat our young," she observed coolly, as her face revealed her agitation.

Johnny again realized the differences in their age. "Calm down now Pumpkin, they're good people. Like everyone else they are afraid of what they're unaccustomed to. What they don't know often impedes what they could experience if they would just keep an open mind. Marks, especially church folks, don't usually wind up with freak show entertainers for son-in-laws." Johnny looked at her and continued with that ever-steady way he had about him, "You and I know what a stand-up guy Happy is but the Lomillers had to discover that for themselves."

With a woman's appreciation for planning, Pumpkin started firing again, "How long are they going to be here? Where are they going to stay? Happy and Greta's trailer is scarcely big enough for the two of them to sleep in," she said, with a worried look.

Johnny, hoping to end what to him was a boring and unnecessary conversation declared, "That's the interesting part of this arrangement. It seems that they recently acquired a small travel trailer. According to Happy, the Lomillers are going to pull on the lot and live like carneys."

Pumpkin burst out laughing. "Happy better keep them away from the joints. Those agents will take all their money. It would be terrible if they had to borrow money to move to the next spot," She was really laughing now.

"Can we just stop all this speculation and talk about us?" Johnny asked, as he pulled Pumpkin close to him.

Pumpkin was still laughing at the thought of the newest members of the carnival having to borrow money to move on. "What did you have in mind?"

With It—For It—and Up Against It

"Well for starters, it might be nice to take Happy and Greta to a decent supper club. Sorta celebrate their recent marriage," he said thoughtfully.

Pumpkin responded in an excited tone. "I've thought about some kind of gift for them but I wasn't sure what they might need."

Johnny had absolutely no idea about such matters. "Don't ask me, I haven't got a clue." He playfully pulled Pumpkin closer. "I know, what about a set of socket wrenches? Happy is always working on something. I'm sure he could find a use for them."

Pumpkin did not find his suggestion appropriate or entertaining. "Be serious, this is an opportunity for you and I to do something really nice for our friends."

Their light banter was interrupted by the organ music on the merry-go-round. Johnny looked at his watch. "Looks like it's time to spring."

For a moment, Pumpkin's face filled with disappointment. There never seemed to be enough time for them to be together. "Guess you need to go to work, huh?" Pumpkin asked, as they walked back toward the front gate.

Johnny placed his arm around her shoulder hugged her close. "You know the routine. The music sounds, the marks come around and hopefully money abounds."

Pumpkin, amused at his silly sayings advised, "You best forget about any career moves that include words and rhymes. You are the worst part-time poet I ever heard." They had one final laugh before they

With It—For It—and Up Against It

went their separate ways. It was getting harder and harder for them to spend time apart.

Silvia was looking out the window when Pumpkin got back to the trailer. Silvia told Pumpkin of the morning tragedy and all that had followed Dixie's arrival. Silvia smiled and informed Pumpkin, "We've had prayer and the reading of the word. However, it was a lot different than I had planned." Silvia starred toward the bedroom where Dixie was resting.

Pumpkin was about to speak when they both saw Dixie walking up the hallway toward them. Silvia could see the rest had done her a lot of good. Under the circumstances she didn't look all that bad.

Her slow distraught movements revealed the dreaded expectations. Dixie tried to smile. Her first words affirmed her grieving heart. "Have they found Pollock?"

Silvia placed a comforting arm around her. "Not yet, but there's a good chance with each passing hour he'll be found alive and improving." Silvia's tone was filled with optimism.

Pumpkin took Dixie's hands and squeezing them softly offered her support. "Oh Dixie, I'm so sorry you've had to go through this terrible ordeal. If there is anything I can do to help, please tell me." The tears in Pumpkin's eyes rolled down her cheeks.

Overwhelmed by the kindness of the Browns, Dixie was so affected she could only manage an appreciative hug.

Silvia, whose motherly instincts had taken control by this time, ushered Dixie to the couch. "You need to eat. I realize that's the last thing you feel like doing, but I'm certain you'll feel better if you will eat a little something."

Pumpkin followed her mother's initiative and immediately opened the refrigerator and began preparing cold cuts and a light salad. Dixie wanted to protest but she knew Silvia was right.

Pumpkin placed the food in front of Dixie. She encouraged her to try and eat something. "Do the best you can. Anything you can get down will help to strengthen you." Pumpkin continued to speak kindly to her while she tidied up the counter space. When she finished her cleaning and told her mother she was going to check on Dad and Dallas. "Is there anything else I can do?

Sylvia laid an affectionate hand on Pumpkin's shoulder. "There is one thing: ask your Daddy if he ordered anymore pineapple concentrate? The last I checked we didn't have enough to make it through next week," Pumpkin admired her mother's faith. Even in the middle of this terrible day, Silvia's trust in God allowed her to take care of her own as well as others.

Malcolm was sitting under the large canvas awning attached to the office trailer. The breeze was cool and the lawn chair he was sitting in was most comfortable. The fragrant aroma of a hand-rolled Monte Cristo Cuban cigar swirled about his head. The taste and texture in his mouth was as familiar as an old friend.

The midway was filling up and it looked like the weather was going to cooperate. He had thoughts of walking around the midway just to check on things.

Normally, Pollock would be out and about. Oddly enough, he'd not seen him all day.

As he was contemplating this unusual circumstance, Easy Money walked in under the awning. Malcolm looked at him briefly, wondering how someone so small and delicate looking could endure the long hours and hard work of the carnival life.

Everyone agreed Easy Money was made out of grit and gristle. No matter the challenge, there was no quit in him. It was his handmade Mexican boots that set him apart, always polished and shined. They were bright red with black strips of leather carved in the likeness of eagles that capped the toes and heels. Because of his lack of height, the heels were an extra two inches thick, elevating his slight stature and his even smaller ego.

They exchanged greetings and Malcolm asked, "Easy Money, I wonder if you would mind doing me a favor?"

"Why no, boss. What do you need?" Easy Money quickly inquired.

"It's Pollock, I haven't seen him all day." Malcolm's tone was serious, more so than usual. "I want you to try to find him. The first place you might look is his trailer. Let me know when you find him." Malcolm took a long pull on his cigar and turned back to enjoy his few moments of peace.

"I'll be back as soon as I know something," Easy Money promised. He hurried off to find Pollock. This was a curious situation.

Pollock had finished the fifth of Jack Daniel's and passed out on the couch. Easy Money knocked hard on his door. There was no answer. He stepped down from the trailer step and was about to leave when he heard a loud gasping sound. He pulled on the door handle. The door swung open easily, revealing Pollock's large body piled on the couch.

Easy Money quietly stepped inside. The rancid smell of alcohol and second-hand smoke was stacked up against the ceiling. He immediately noticed a blood-encrusted towel encircling Pollock's head. The stain's blood-red hue, intensified against the white towel, screamed for someone to unveil the scandal and shame that was hidden beneath its folds.

Pollock's gurgling gasps signaled the indifferent slumber of an alcohol-induced stupor. "He ain't going nowhere soon," Easy Money said softly. Knowing the power and passion of the big man, Easy Money wondered what freight train had run him down. His face had somehow escaped the trauma that advertised its fury in embedded emblems of pain inscribed in his scalp. "He ain't pretty," Easy Money mumbled. "But then, he never was."

It was hot inside the small trailer and it showed on Pollock's sweat soaked clothing. Easy Money located a window fan and turned it on. The sweltering heat, repulsed by the determined intentions of the window's circulating fan, filled the atmosphere with scattered pockets of air that exuded heat like a smoldering inferno.

He rolled open the vents in the ceiling and checked to make sure all the windows were open. Knowing of nothing else to do, Easy Money let himself out,

With It—For It—and Up Against It

closed the door behind him and headed back toward the office.

Snag Hughes and Willie, the electrician, were huddled up in the floor of the hot wagon shooting dice. Easy Money walked in just as Willie had made his point. Shooting dice was the nearest thing to religion that Willie knew. He loved the little black spotted ivory cubes. They seemed to love him in return. Howling with gleeful delight, he swept up Snag's money from the floor with his calloused hand and declared, "Come to Ol' Willie you lovely works of the engravers art. They gonna have to run that U S mint twenty four hours a day if you keep this up," Willie teased, as Snag threw up his hands in defeat.

Snag looked up at Easy Money and asked, "What about you, money man? You got any left over cash you'd like to contribute? You can sure have my place. I'm all through," Snag declared good-naturedly.

Easy knew better. He wasn't about to gamble with Willie. He sure wasn't gonna shoot craps with him. "Naw," he replied, "I just came by to see if you boys knew what happened to Pollock?"

"What do you mean?" Snag asked, as he looked at Easy Money with a searching look.

"Well, I'll tell you what I know." Easy Money answered. "Malcolm sent me looking for him. It seems he's been nowhere to be seen since last night. I found him all right. He looked like he'd been sacking wildcats. His head looked like someone had beat on it like a drum. He was bloody and bad drunk. I'll tell you something else," Easy said confidently, "he ain't gonna be happy when he wakes up."

Everyone in the hot wagon roared with laughter. "It's too bad he has to wake up," Snag observed, as his face suddenly turned from mirth to mean.

"Hold on now," Willie advised, "Don't even think about ending his recovery. His day is coming, sounds to me like it's already arrived."

Like any place else the carnival lot embraces gossip among its own. In less than an hour the battered physical condition of Pollock was known up and down the midway.

When the glad good news that he was alive reached the Brown's trailer the sounds of celebration reverberated toward heaven. Everyone in the trailer was rejoicing and giving God praise. Dixie was certain God had provided a way of escape.

Always the practical mother, Silvia formulated a plan to secure Dixie a change of clothes. She wanted everything possible done to insure that Malcolm never learned of the tragic events of this day. Some things are just better if they can be buried with the past. "Old things are passed away, all things become new."

CHAPTER 11

∽

Pollock lived an uncluttered life, so he required few creature comforts. He did have one personal grooming habit that brought him great satisfaction and pleasure, no matter the circumstance. Regardless of the inconvenience and bother, he was always clean-shaven. When possible, he especially enjoyed the sharp strokes of a straight razor skillfully employed by a professional barber.

He was returning from the city where he had obtained some replacement parts for the fly-o-plane. Never one to miss an opportunity to indulge his passion, he had found the nearest barbershop on his way out. His face tingled from a recent splash of after-shave. This preceded a wonderful moisturizing lotion that had completed his brief but tantalizing visit in the barber's chair.

It seemed such and odd depiction of his otherwise macho image. One might even conclude that his meticulous attention to his face was almost effeminate. It was especially curious when one examined his blunt features. Pollock was hard and severe, far from handsome. All of his efforts did little to improve his appearance.

It had been more than a week now since Shorty Yeager had dragged him inside the trailer. He had explained his altered appearance by declaring he had fallen down a flight of steps near the Grandstand entrance. Nobody believed him, but nobody contradicted him either.

His resentment for Dixie and Malcolm was growing day by day. He had made a few inquiries about employment, as he fully expected to be dismissed. If not immediately, he was certain he would be let go when the season was over.

His reputation as a ride superintendent was known and respected. His inability to get along with his fellow employees was also common knowledge.

Arriving back at the lot with the necessary parts in hand he walked toward the fly-o-plane. Nancy Wright, hurrying toward the front gate, almost bumped into him. He looked at her in amusement and said, "Hey, Double Bottom, what's the hurry?"

Puffing from her hip-gyrating rapid gait she rumbled on and called out in passing, "I'm headed to the Grandstand. I haven't got time to talk to you," she wheezed, increasing her stride.

She could hear the Grandstand announcer's final call. "Get your tickets now, ri— —ght now. Ladies and gentlemen, children of all ages, it's big-time auto racing under the covered grandstand. Open wheel, triple AAA big car racing. Get your tickets now, ri—-ght now. Time trials start in ten minutes," the announcer declared, as Double Bottom purchased her ticket. She was not just a fan; she was a fanatic. She loved open wheel racing. Her heart rate increased to near lethal limits at the mere sound of the Indianapolis roadsters. They were hot lapping the big cars in preparation for qualifying, their engine's furious exhaust note howled its statement of power and speed. The ferocious rumbling of the Offenhouser, Ranger and Miller power plants roused and stimulated her to lightheaded heights of crazed deliriousness.

A veteran spectator of dirt track racing, Nancy carefully selected a seat where she could escape the mud and later the dust that would find its way to particular areas of the Grandstand. Her rapid heart rate had slowed a little as she endeavored to calm down. Beneath her seat was her ever-present purse, if you could call it that. The dimensions would easily place it in the category of a suitcase, a well-worn suitcase — it was heavy and dirty and old.

Contained within its confines was a large thermos bottle full of gin, an assortment of candy bars and nuts, chips and packs and packs of cigarettes. One of the just-in-case items was a 22-caliber pistol. It wasn't loaded and it didn't even look like it would work. There was no compact, no comb, no lipstick, nothing that would cater to the vanity of a woman. Nancy Wright had long ago stopped caring what she looked like.

Being the sister of the show owner had its rewards. The merry-go-round ticket box was presently being occupied by Shorty Yeager himself. He

With It—For It—and Up Against It

would be required to sell tickets until she returned. She chuckled out loud as she thought of his discomfort and depression.

Inside the cubicle known as Double Bottom's plantation, Shorty fumed and fussed. With listless movements, he dispensed the tickets with an air of pessimism and protest. Shorty fancied himself to be an executive type, a man of untapped possibilities. He felt his assignment in the merry-go-round ticket box was beneath his managerial skills and did little to enhance his inflated ego.

Down on the Midway, a crowd had lined up in front of the Geek Show ticket box. The Geek Show was a great crowd pleaser. The act inside was so outrageous it had been banned in all but a few states. The Geek Show was and is a testimony to the entrepreneurial abilities of man, which in this case, reached an all-time low in the mad pursuit of cash at any cost.

Inside the dimly lit tent was a 6-foot by 8-foot cage. Revealed within the interior of that steel-barred protector of the public was what was described as a Congolian tribesman. The audience was told he was captured in the darkest regions of Africa. In reality, he's some mother's slow-witted son, born and raised in Toledo, Ohio or some other small place; a discarded member of the human race, Innocent and unaware this poor creature was. A used and abused pound of flesh exhibited for the delight of the perverse, nothing but a moneymaker for his undeserving masters.

Presented as a dark, disheveled, long-haired savage, dressed in a loincloth, he scurries about on all fours. Glass containers, strategically placed around the cage to attract the attention of the audience, are filled with frogs and snakes. Various colored chickens cluck and crow, pecking the floor of the cage for grain that had been indiscriminately scattered about.

Without warning, the serene atmosphere accelerates into alarm. The geek, presented as the savage tribesman from the Dark Continent, opens the glass jar, grasps a frog and shoves it in his mouth. Madness is on exhibition without apology. Suddenly he swallows the frog and then regurgitates him. Many in the audience, who have fared sumptuously on hot dogs and other carnival fare, throw up as well.

This litmus test for insanity doesn't stop here. After sucking on the heads of the slithering snakes, he bites and rips the head off of a chicken and drinks its blood. This shocking and titillating exhibition of madness never fails to clear the tent. The paying public would all agree, for once they got more than their money's worth. As quickly as one group clears out another group crowds in.

A few hours later, down the Midway from the Geek Show, Red O'Grady had just concluded the last bally for the final fight of the night. The day had been long and tiring. Sitting down on the front of the platform with his legs dangling over the edge, he reflects on events of the day.

He was more than a little curious about Pollock's ridiculous explanation. Those swollen abrasions on his head were not the result of a fall. Someone had played rootie toot toot on his noggin, fast and hard. But who? Other than himself and his stable of fighters he couldn't think of more than two others who were even capable of going to war with Pollock. Snag Hughes could have done it, or maybe it was Johnny Palmer. Problem was, the wounds didn't look like he'd been in a regular fistfight. In a regular fight noses get broken, eyes get gouged and blackened. No, this was something definitely out of the ordinary. Whoever whacked on his head is a good friend of mine and everyone else around here, Red thought, and a huge smile lit up his face.

"What kind of mischief are you plotting," Claude Brimbly asked, as Red continued to smile. "Aw, I was just setting here wondering whether the rain was gonna hurt the rhubarb crop in Amarillo or not." They both laughed at his outrageous statement of nonsense.

"Say Red, everybody's talking about Pollock's terrible *fall*," Claude stated, with a sarcastic tone. Warming to the absurdity of Pollock's statement Claude said, "I heard some of the ride boys were gonna hold a service in front of those Grandstand steps. They wanted to honor each treaded step for the aggravation and injury they inflicted on The Mighty Wright Shows beloved ride superintendent."

Red laughed appreciatively. He always enjoyed Claude's brutal frivolity. He looked at Claude and said, "I always had hopes of getting him in the ring. Dadblamed if it don't look like someone beat me to it."

Claude and Red had been friends for many years. He knew Red's highly-regarded athletic abilities were declining, but he was also confident that with half his skills Red was still more than an even bet to defeat Pollock. "Tell the truth, Red," Claude insisted. "You put some God-awful wrestling hold on him and squeezed his head until those holes popped up, didn't you?" Claude pointed an accusing finger at him and demanded, "Well, didn't you?"

Red relished the thought. "No, but I wish I had. The only reason I didn't was because I never got a chance."

"Whatta you say we settle up at the office and then go get something to eat," Claude suggested, as Red climbed down from the platform.

"Are you asking me out?" Red inquired good-naturedly, as they walked toward the office.

The line at the check-out window of the carnival office was starting to lengthen as the ticket sellers brought in the night's take.

Double Bottom wobbled up to the steps more unsteady than usual. She reeked of stale smoke and gin. Somehow an empty potato chip bag had attached itself to the front of her blouse. It looked like an accessorized joke, except there was nothing funny about Double Bottom's condition.

She'd had a full day. The thrilling excitement of the auto races coupled with a double allowance of gin had all but immobilized her. She was dead drunk and didn't know it.

Easy Money knew it. He felt sorry for her. Why would you do something like that to yourself, he wondered?

Swaying like a palm tree in a hard wind, she struggled to stay upright. "Nancy, let me help you," Easy Money said kindly.

With It—For It—and Up Against It

Unaccustomed to hearing her first name she turned toward him almost gracefully and then fell. Her eyes wide, she searched his face with a sweet but comical expression.

He stooped down and struggled to get her in an upright position. There was so much of her and so little of him he really didn't know where to start.

"Perhaps I can be of some assistance," Johnny said, as he clasped his arms around Double Bottom. With what appeared to be little effort, he stood her erect. Easy Money couldn't even comprehend how much power and strength Johnny had just exhibited.

Easy Money spoke to her as though she was a child. "Nancy, you need to sit down under the awning and let me take your tickets and money bag to the window."

"You go ahead and see about her," Johnny instructed. "I'll see that she gets checked out."

"No one but Malcolm ever calls me Nancy." Her tongue was so thick and her mind so muddled, conversation was real tricky just now.

Easy Money stood quietly as she continued. "You sure do have on some pretty boots. I had a pair of red boots when I was a girl. You don't talk much do you?" she asked, as she struck a match and tried to line it up with a cigarette she had jabbed in her mouth.

Realizing she was never going to make it, he steadied her hand as she lit the cigarette and inhaled deeply.

"Man, you should have been with me today." Her speech was getting even more slurred. "I went to the big car races. All the best drivers showed up. It was one fine race." Her eyes began to droop.

Easy Money knew it wouldn't be long until she passed out. Seeing Johnny descending the office steps he called out, "Hey Johnny, would you mind helping me get her to her trailer?"

"No, of course not." Johnny realized what they needed was some feminine assistance. "Tell you what, Pumpkin's waiting for me at the custard trailer. I'll go get her. She can help us get her home." Johnny turned and hurried down the Midway.

After enlisting Pumpkin's help, the bedding down of Nancy Wright was accomplished with a minimum of bother. Easy Money, having exercised his duty as a Good Samaritan and satisfied that Nancy was comfortable and safe, said good night.

Johnny hadn't seen Pumpkin all day. Standing there under a full moon he was startled at how indescribably beautiful she was. As if pierced by cupid's arrow, his pulse began to race. Desire and passion, vigorous and intense surged through his soul in pent up waves of ardent fervor.

"I don't suppose you'd care to go get something to eat would you?" Pumpkin was keenly aware of Johnny's amorous attention.

A reckless grin appeared on Johnny's face. "No, but you look way too good and way too desirable to be safe here. Whatta you say to a romantic meal in the ostentatious surrounding of Bill Charity's cook house."

Pumpkin summoned her best Puritan voice and batted her eyes. "Why yes, of course. The ambience

With It—For It—and Up Against It

of friends, fried onions and festive profanity are the perfect touch to any well-planned date." She loved when he teased her. She took hold of his arm, on top of the world, walking to Bill Charity's cookhouse. She couldn't be happier.

As they walked along, the she longed to give Johnny the low down about Pollock's battered appearance. They had said nothing about it between the two of them. She also knew by experience that he would never mention it. One of the many noble qualities of his character was his aversion to gossip. As difficult as it was, she remained silent, electing not to press the issue.

The cookhouse was as she had described it, loud, libertarian and licentious. On the good side, the onions were freshly fried.

Looking for a place to sit, Red O'Grady waved them over to his table. Claude Brimbly was happily gnawing on a pork chop bone. "Pay him no mind," Red said, as Claude paused to come up for air. Claude was a very proper and meticulous man except for his appetite. He was a gastronomical junkie. He loved to eat. His expansive girth testified to his passion for food.

Johnny and Pumpkin sat down, gave their order and watched as Red pushed back what was left of a very rare T-bone. Red, bold and curious, wasted no time in satisfying his curiosity concerning Pollock. "Johnny, what do you know about Pollock's hammered-up head?

Johnny was ill at ease, knowing his name had been thrown about in the rumor mill. "Nothing, absolutely nothing. Why would I?" Bill set their orders down in front of them and he was thankful for the momentary distraction.

"No reason." Red watched Johnny carefully for any body language that might say different.

After his judicious attack on the pork chop bone, Claude unable to garner even one tiny delicious sliver more, looked up and said, "It sure as hell wasn't me!" If there had been an indelicate moment it quickly passed as everyone at the table laughed at Claude's hilarious denial.

Before their laughter subsided, Malcolm and Dixie walked through the front of the cookhouse and sat down at a recently vacated table next to Red's.

"Well, hey Pumpkin," Dixie squealed in a delighted tone.

Pumpkin, equally glad to see her new Christian friend replied, "Hey yourself, Dixie. I sure am happy to see you two." She waved a slender hand at Malcolm.

That was as far as the pleasantries got. Unbeknownst to Dixie, Pollock had been stalking her.

Angry and determined to have his revenge, he had decided he didn't really care whether he finished the season or not. His job be damned, tonight someone would pay.

Lumbering up to Malcolm's table, he looked across the room into the amused eyes of Red O'Grady. Before Pollock could speak, Red taunted him. "Hello, bad boy. Are you about healed up? I'm thinking you need a little more training in the fine art of tussling."

Pollock's face turned blood red as his temper ignited into flames of hatred and spite. "That might not be a job you're capable of carrying out, old man." Pollock planned his next move.

Red snorted in disgust. "I can turn the ring lights on right now Sonny, unless you're afraid."

This wasn't going the way Pollock had intended. He had come in the cookhouse with the expressed purpose of imposing his will on Malcolm and Dixie. He wanted to publicly humiliate them both. Catching a glimpse of Johnny Palmer's face, he decided a confrontation with him was his way out. "Hey Palmer," he said loudly. "Everywhere I go folks are saying you busted up my head. You wouldn't know anything about that, now would you?"

Before Johnny could answer, Pollock spoke even louder. "Naw, that would take some guts and you're just a sissified pretty boy." Every syllable was punctuated with nastiness, daring Johnny to respond.

Johnny got up from the table, ignoring Pollock's childish accusations. He looked at Pumpkin and said, "We better be going." He took her hand and quickly walked out of the front of the cookhouse.

They hadn't walked more than ten feet when he heard Red shout, "Look out, Johnny!" He pushed Pumpkin aside and turned just in time to duck under a huge right-handed haymaker. The fury of Pollock's punch sizzled as it passed by within inches of his head. Had his sucker punch succeeded, Johnny could have very easily been knocked out.

With It—For It—and Up Against It

Without thinking, Johnny locked his wrist, balled his fist and buried his punch into Pollock's rock-hard stomach. He struck with such force a strange whistling noise sounded an embarrassing note of surprise as Pollock found himself seated on the ground. By now everyone in the cookhouse had surrounded the combatants. Red looked happily at Claude. "Pollock's in for it now. He's used to beating up drunken ride boys and local plow hands. He's jumped himself out a real scrapper. I've watched Johnny — the way he walks on the balls of his feet —the way he moves. There's ring ropes and a heavy bag in his past. Pollock's about to find it out." Red howled with anticipated delight.

Pollock got up on one knee and looked at Johnny with a new sense of respect. He struggled to his feet, groaning and mumbling, "This ain't gonna be as easy as I first thought. You should have stomped me while I was down, that was your only hope. Now, you're just gonna get the hell beat out of you. I'm gonna break you up. When I get through you ain't gonna be pretty anymore." Pollock rubbed his muscular forearms.

Not intimidated by Pollock's boisterous threats, Johnny grinned at him. "Are you going to fight or visit? All I've experienced so far is a lot of talk."

This wasn't a choreographed stunt, staged to meet the expectations of an undefeated belligerent bully. It was a fight, possibly to the death. So far, Johnny wasn't cooperating. Pollock had bloodied, broken and battered every man he had gotten his hands on. He was confident the outcome of this fight would be no different. His intent was to wrestle him to the ground, knowing that if he got a hold of him he was going to break some bones. His power had never failed him.

Pollock rushed in with murderous fury. When he reached the correct distance Johnny coiled his hips, inside his shoes he curled his toes as though he was trying to grip the ground. He locked his wrist, turned his fist over and Pollock's face exploded as Johnny's uppercut found its mark. A look of unbelief filled Pollock's eyes as the ground slammed into the back of his head. Blood was spurting from his nose. Two more minutes and his eyes, already turning black, would begin to swell shut. Shamed and surprised, his breath was coming in loud gasps. His zeal for combat was waning. A little unsteady, Pollock got to his feet. His broken nose was already beginning to impede his breathing.

Johnny felt the trauma and power of that uppercut all the way up his shoulder. He was surprised Pollock was still conscious. He couldn't remember ever punching anyone that hard.

"Is that the best you can do?" Pollock snorted and spit. To his dismay, a large puddle of blood appeared on the ground. Carefully, he circled Johnny, looking for an opportunity to grab hold of him.

Johnny's voice was low and cold, his eyes calm and confident. "Tonight, I'm repaying you for the beating you gave my agent in the G top."

Roaring with depraved hostility, Pollock like a mad bull, once again rushed in. This time, Johnny stood his ground. Upon impact, he used Pollock's weight and strength against him. He dropped, rolled and heaved, sending Pollock hurling through the air. His mighty mass of muscle and bone impacted the earth with the dismembering jolt of a falling meteorite. There were broken bones as expected. But this time, for the first time, they were Pollock's.

Pollock, all but unconscious, had no wind and no fight left in him. Johnny straddled his chest and began to beat him unmercifully.

He rained down his adjudged punishment quick and severe. Professional and without pity, he hammered his face. By now Pollock didn't resemble anything, let alone a person. He was knocked out and had been out, many thought long enough.

Someone said, "That's enough, Johnny!" Riled and abandoned to his baser nature Johnny growled out a warning. "I'll decide when he's had enough, you better get back." He continued to exact his revenge.

Composed and concerned, Red knelt down beside Johnny and quietly spoke to him. "Kid, you've gotta stop. You're gonna kill him if you don't."

Somehow, Red's fatherly advice broke through the thermal barrier of outrage. The red haze of brutal fury lifted. Johnny stood up, took no notice of Pollock or the crowd and without a word, walked away.

Pumpkin ran after him calling his name. There was no response. "Johnny, for heaven's sake, where are you going?" Pumpkin had never seen him like this before. She wasn't sure what would happen next.

Red followed after Pumpkin. With a gladiator's knowledge of men, he said, "Let him go right now.

With It—For It—and Up Against It

He needs some time to himself. He'll come around when he's ready."

"I don't understand," She continued to call his name.

"Well," Red said, "it's like this, not being an intemperate man, Johnny has just plumbed the depths of his own anger and rage. Right about now he's struggling to understand his loss of composure. He'll be alright, just give him a little time." Red walked back to where Claude was standing.

Claude's voice was excited. "Man, you was right. It was no contest. They still haven't been able to get Pollock on his feet."

"Has he regained consciousness yet?" Red inquired.

"I'm not certain. I do know somebody said along with his nose his jaw was broken."

"He's busted up, that's for sure," Red said, as a crowd of men attempted to decide what to do next.

Malcolm now recovered from the dramatic violence of the last few minutes made the decision. "Load what's left of him in the show panel truck and take him to the hospital. He's definitely going to need some medical assistance." His tone was frigid.

Standing next to Dixie, Noble, without any compassion in his voice said, "He's been asking for a whipping for a long time. He finally met his match and more. Man, did he ever!"

Malcolm looked at Noble in full agreement. "I don't want to ever see him on this Midway again. Pay him off. I want you to include his end of the season bonus. It's worth it to be rid of him. Tell him to never come around Dixie or me again. If he does, tell him I'll put holes in him a pie pan won't cover." His voice was edged with smoldering wrath.

Taken back by Malcolm's enraged instructions Noble quietly promised to take care of it. Malcolm and Dixie, holding hands turned and walked down the Midway.

CHAPTER 12

The conversation around the carnival continued to have as its center what was now called, 'the big fight.'

Anxious to move on and unwilling to serve as a heroic role model, Johnny was hoping his celebrated exploits would soon be cloaked in obscurity. He felt ill at ease with all of the unsolicited attention. Everyone with an axe to grind had elected him as their advocate. The list of those who had personally lavished him with praise for settling their grievances, along with his own, seemed endless. All agreed this week was a lot happier than last week.

A favorite of most of the ride boys, Snag Hughes had been promoted to ride superintendent. Everyone and everything on the lot was operating without a hitch. The Midway had taken on an almost festive atmosphere. The fact that the season was almost over contributed to the upbeat attitudes exemplified by most of the carneys.

Noble had carried out Malcolm's instructions as directed. His visit to the hospital revealed Pollock was mending physically. His brash, conceited ego was not so fortunate. The ease in which Johnny had demonstrated his superior skills as a fighter had left him confused and uncertain. Still big and powerful, he was no longer the tyrant of terror. His bones would mend, but all the bully had been beaten out of him. He was docile as a little lamb.

Noble had surprised Pollock. He had not expected any visitors. He was equally surprised to receive his end of the season bonus. He had been certain that part of his pay had been forfeited. Knowing Malcolm as he did, he should have known he would be more than fair. Pollock was, however, taken aback by Malcolm's brutal promise of punishment and the possibility of loss of life if he set foot on the lot. He had no intention of returning. He had been savaged and shamed. The caustic harassment of his peers was too much agitation and agony to even contemplate.

The few minutes necessary to complete their transaction of cash and warning of calamity was extremely awkward for both of them. Noble almost felt sorry for the big Pollock. His entire way of life had been forfeited in one underhanded attack that he had foolishly initiated. In one humiliating moment his weaknesses had been exposed and his reputation destroyed. The chances were good he'd be a better person. Even he should be able to learn from his mistakes. The question is, can he find happiness without all the bluster and belligerence? Some men are bullies by choice. They don't want to change.

Concluding his assigned task, without a friendly word, Noble said goodbye for what he hoped was the last time.

Back on the Midway, Johnny was trying to avoid any conversation pertaining to the fight or the enthusiastic interest it had engendered about his past history as a fighter. He shunned the numerous questions and inquiries with the same reply, "It's over, let's talk about something else." He had refused to discuss that night with anyone, including Pumpkin. It was time to move on.

After a few days, when the time was right, he relented and had a lengthy private conversation with Red. He was the only one he felt could understand the mindset that had birthed his blind rage. It was his wise council that helped him come to terms with the feelings of shame and remorse he'd experienced when he realized he'd lost control. If not for Red, he might have killed Pollock. It was odd when he considered how close that night of violence had brought them. He would never look at Red in the same way. They had bonded in a moment of battle that had rescued him from the depths of unmasked ferocity.

Never having had a father, he now considered Red his mentor and unfailing friend. It was a role Red was pleased to accept. Johnny Palmer was everything and more than Red had hoped for in the son he never had.

The days got shorter and the nights much cooler. The end of the season arrived almost unannounced.

The speaker box hanging from the driver side window allowed the brisk and biting night air entrance into the comfortable confines of Johnny's Buick. It was the last spot of the carnival season and he and Pumpkin had decided to take in the sci-fi thriller at the local drive-in theatre.

Opening tomorrow, the carnival would begin working the final fair of the schedule. All thoughts about business and life on the lot were lost as they viewed the appalling aliens appearing on the silver screen. These impudent invaders from Mars were secretly taking over the bodies of unsuspecting civilians. Their diabolic plot to take over the world seemed to be succeeding. Only a few of the townspeople stood between them and world dominance.

Pumpkin cuddled up a little closer to Johnny as the fiendish intruders reeked havoc among the unsuspecting victims.

Tonight would be a night to remember. Johnny had decided he could wait no longer. A dimly lit three star restaurant may have been more appropriate but his mind was made up. Tonight he would ask Pumpkin to marry him. In his right hand pocket was an engagement ring. Expensive. of fine quality clarity and more than two carats. He had bought it eight weeks ago from a booster – boosters were individuals who sold items obtained from unknown sources. It could be almost anything from almost anywhere. One thing was certain, the police wouldn't be welcome shoppers. Boosters usually worked out of the trunk of their car.

Often known by many of the carneys, they didn't travel with the carnival. They would appear and park on the back side of the midway. The word would

With It—For It—and Up Against It

quietly and quickly get out among the carneys that they had merchandise. Most of their stock was of the highest quality and was sold for far less than half of its retail value – clothes, furs, appliances, TVs, watches and jewelry of all kinds.

Carneys thought no more of obtaining possessions in this way than marks did of patronizing their local shops.

Pumpkin pulled Johnny's face away from viewing the carnage on the screen and asked teasingly, "Are you a scaredy cat?"

Johnny faked an expression of fear. "Yes, I was just about to open the door and run. My frightened feelings struck me in the oddest place — my stomach. It has been growling for over an hour."

"My goodness," Pumpkin sympathized, "you poor thing, you need food to calm your anxiety and alarm." Pumpkin continued this charade and asked, "Can Mama's big boy go to the refreshment bar alone or must she go with him?"

Johnny laughed and asked as he opened the door, "What can I bring you? You must be hungry. I'm certain all that screaming and hiding your face has created a need for nutrition."

Pumpkin, in an imperious tone, both polite and pretended, gave him her order and then shoved him out the door. With an ambiguous affirmation she said, "Go alone little man, you can do it."

He laughed and shut the door.

A little while later, Johnny returned to the car. He had a found a lot at the refreshment bar to his liking. Pumpkin aided his entrance by swinging the passen-

With It—For It—and Up Against It

ger's door open. Once inside, he began disbursing his gastronomical delights with missionary zeal. It was obvious he had purchased plenty.

"Dig in," he encouraged as he continued to arrange and spread the varied tasty treats. Pumpkin was always amazed at his gargantuan appetite. She ate very little. She really wasn't hungry.

With slow and deliberate competence, the food began to disappear. There was no smacking, impolite attack by some glutton out of control food freak; it was more of a measured consuming by a man with a metabolism of a locomotive.

Pumpkin looked at him in the half-light and marveled at the great God who had provided her with such a wonderful man — sleek and supple, muscular and manly, well mannered and kind.

"What is it?" Johnny asked.

His question cut through her thoughtful gaze. "I was just wondering if all that food would be enough," she said as she patted his rock hard stomach.

The movie ended in victory as the townspeople with Yankee ingenuity defeated the vicious visitors from outer space.

Little was said on the way back to the lot. Pumpkin happily sat close to Johnny and looked out the windshield as the sights of night passed in a blur. It had been a wonderful night.

Johnny pulled up in front of Pumpkin's trailer and shut off the engine on the Buick. They sat silently for a time, then, tenderly he took her in his arms. Her lips were soft and yielding. Her face beautiful in the moonlight was innocent and compliant, irresistible.

The passion of their embrace was electrifying. She was warm and inviting. Their souls melted into one white-hot eruption of pent up emotions.

Exploring the phenomenon of wistful desires loosed, they lost themselves in the volcanic intensity of the moment. Alarmed at her own loss of resolve, Pumpkin managed to quell the blissful force of enchantment and ecstasy. Their dizzying exploration into celestial pleasures of paradise would have to wait. With sweet restraint, she pulled away.

Breaking the silence and the awkwardness of the moment, with a lopsided grin, Johnny asked, "Where in the hell am I?"

Pumpkin laughed nervously and replied, "I'm not sure. Do you feel like you've been hypnotized? I do," she declared as she rolled down the window and took a deep breath.

"Well here's something else to elevate your heart rate," Johnny said, as he retrieved the engagement ring from his pocket, knowing now was the moment.

Placing the ring upon her finger, Johnny said, "You are all I've every longed for in a women. Will you be my wife?"

Rendered almost breathless, Pumpkin could scarcely believe her ears. She had waited for this moment all of her life. Now the man of her dreams had asked her to marry him. God had surely saved the best until now.

"Yes, oh, yes, I'll marry you! I've never loved anyone but you!" she declared and fell into his arms.

With It—For It—and Up Against It

The last days of the fair flew by as Johnny and Pumpkin planned for a winter wedding. They both agreed they wanted to continue living on the road. The life of a carney was in their blood. They were happy to be a part of the old carney slogan, "With it, for it and up against it."

Happy and Greta's winter work was laid out before them. They were going to assist her parents in framing a PDQ mug joint. Mr. Lomiller loved taking pictures. Next year he'd be doing it for the fair goers. Apparently, life on the carnival wasn't so bad after all!

Malcolm and Dixie were happily anticipating their first child. If a boy, they planned to name him Joel, after the mighty Prophet of God, if a girl, Sarah, to remind them of the faithfulness of God.

Agitatin' Bill rolled the sidewall of the merry-go-round in a tight bundle and placed it in a large canvass bag. It was the last time it would be used this year. Another season had come and gone.

Challenges, changes and circumstances had filled his and everyone's lives with the ups and downs of the Merry-go-round.

Until next season . . .
The End

Printed in the United States
48988LVS00001B